MW00916161

MURDER BY THE BAY

SUSIE FASBINDER

Dedication

To George and Kate, my inspirations...

Contents

Prologue

Lucas was fourteen when he started working after school at the Morrison's Chapel and Crematorium by the Bay on Sharon Street in the town of Fairfax in Marin County, California, just eleven miles north of the Golden Gate Bridge. He never told his parents he worked at a crematorium after school, and they never asked. It was too morbid to tell his friends.

After a few weeks, he realized, as he swept ashes off the floor and polished the urns full of deceased people's ashes, that he liked being with the dead. They are still people, after all, and he talked to them as he did his job.

They were all great listeners.

1

Meet The Ashes

It's nearly dark. There's a faint ghostly howling of the wind and a strong rustling of the tall trees surrounding a once-magnificent, now broken-down Victorian mansion, the Morrison Chapel and Crematorium by the Bay, as a lanky, sandy-haired teenager barrels up the rickety stairs to the back entrance. He's almost handsome with that bike-accident-made-dimple on his left cheek. Blasting music escapes from his ear buds, as he takes two stairs at a time, still pumped from football practice and eager to get inside. The teenager is Lucas Reilly, aged 14, and he's late for work.

He steps onto the porch. The loud creaking of the floorboards reminds him to walk lightly on the termite-infested floor or he might fall through to whatever he suspects is living-in-wait for him under the funeral home. He does a jump inspired by his tire-to-tire football practice moves to avoid the really bad spots and laughs at himself.

"Coach Neely would love this." His fake dimple lights

up his smile. Safely at the back door, he turns the doorknob. It doesn't turn. "That's strange. The door is always unlocked during work." He tries the doorknob again and knocks on the door.

"Hello, anybody there?" No answer.

Getting no response, he steps over to the unwashed window to the right of the door. As he steps aside, he notices a car with its motor running at the side of the building."Hmm, someone's gotta be inside."

Now at the window, which is too dirty to see through, he takes the bottom of his flannel shirt and makes circles on the window to remove the dirt. He switches from hand to hand and keeps making circles. After the small circles he's made allow him to peek in, he sees that the room is surprisingly empty. Facing the window, he suddenly shivers from a weird sensation, like something crawling up the back of his neck. He puts his hand to his neck, and something cold touches his hand. He jumps back from the window and looks around, thinking someone is there. He's heard the stories of the Morrison murder in the mansion and the ghost that haunts the place.

But when he looks over his shoulder, he's totally alone except for the swirling wind that's picked up some leaves and is making a whooshing sound on the floorboards. He pulls up his flannel shirt collar in defense against the cold. Just pulling it up over his neck makes him feel safer. He takes out his cell phone to assure himself that it's working and checks the time. It's 6:30. He knocks on the window again. Trying to calm himself, he jokingly says, "Open up, it's the police. I know you're in there."

Frustrated, he steps away from the window when— THUD—he hears a sound like a chair falling over. Lucas knocks on the window harder, convinced someone's in there. Then, without warning—BANG—the back door suddenly bursts open and crashes hard against the building wall. Lucas dramatically grabs his chest, thinking he's been shot. He turns ghost white and starts gasping for air. He props himself up against the building and starts patting himself up and down looking for evidence of a bloody gunshot wound. Finding nothing and slowly regulating his breathing, something he learned from that weird yoga retreat his mother forced him to go on for his anxiety, his color comes back into his cheeks. Standing up, he notices that the back door has swung open, and it has smashed into one of the back walls. Taking more deep breaths, Lucas looks around to make sure no one saw him be so uncool. Shaken and with wobbly legs, he carefully walks over to the back door, tugs at it, pulls it from the wall, and walks inside like nothing had happened.

Once inside, he makes his way down a bleak unlit corridor. He opens a door with a "Mortuary Storage Room" sign posted above the door. He flicks on the light and drops his backpack down, which scatters all the ashes on the floor.

"Damn, I always do that." He picks up the backpack, blows off the ashes, and puts it on a shelf. In the dim light he sees rows of empty crematorium urns. He starts to work immediately. He counts all the empty urns and signs off on the inventory clipboard, then walks over to another shelf with three urns that are filled with ashes. These are the urns filled with ashes of loved ones who are still being stored at the mortuary, the so-called unclaimed urns. It feels wrong to Lucas that no one has come to bring them home.

"Hiya, buddies," Lucas says cheerfully. He picks up his polishing cloth, dips it into the silver polish, spreads it on the urn, and reads the inscriptions of the deceased out loud.

"Marianne Holtz." He thinks for a second, "Probably a school teacher." He gives the urn an extra wipe with his cloth, Lucas carefully puts her urn back on the shelf. He picks up the urn next to Marianne. "Hmm, William Ketchum, definitely in real estate."

As he continues to polish... "Willy, right below you is Benjamin Forman, Esquire. I'm guessing a lawyer of some kind. Benny, say hello to Willy and Marianne."

Lucas grins, getting a kick out of introducing the deceased to one another.

Suddenly he hears a loud noise coming from the crematorium room next door. At the same time, Lucas notices beads of water dripping onto the floor. He raises his hand to his forehead and feels the sweat pouring over his face and down his shirt and onto the floor.

"Jeez, it must be two-hundred degrees in here. Someone must have turned on the oven."

Lucas carefully places the urn he's holding back on the shelf.

An unnerving clanging of big cans crashing together and the faint smell of smoke and gasoline permeate the storage room. Lucas turns to face the door and is about to head out to get a grasp of the situation when the handle of the closed door starts to turn on its own. Lucas watches the door handle turn and feels that same shiver he felt outside, but now he's sweating. Sensing real danger, he turns away from the door and walks to the back of the room.

The door squeaks open and heavy footsteps echo across the room. Before he can turn around to see who's there, the room goes pitch black. Thrown into the dark, he steps forward, and feels something hit his head. He crashes into the shelves, then falls to the floor.

When he comes to, the lights are back on and there are ashes all over the floor. Lucas scoops up the ashes and puts what he can back in the overturned urns. Talking to the urns and holding the back of his head, he says, "Sorry, fellas, at least now you have each other." The door is wide open and the smell of gasoline is pungent.

As he turns out the lights, he hears a car screeching away. He locks up and leaves.

Lucas gets home and sneaks up the backstairs to his room. He flops down on his bed, still holding his head. He checks his hand for blood. There's a drop on his hand. He wipes it on his shirt and closes his eyes. He has a whopping headache.

Still lying on his bed in his clothes from yesterday, Lucas's room is flooded in bright morning light. He opens his eyes, then shuts them quickly. He groans. He opens one eye and holds his head.

"Holy cow, what hit me?" His mouth is like sandpaper. He reaches for an old can of soda from his nightstand, takes a swig and sprays it out. It's flat, and there's a bug in the can. He fumbles opening his laptop on his nightstand and sees it's nine a.m. "Ugh! School!" He bolts up. The room spins, but he gets up, takes off his shirt, sniffs a dirty one from the floor, "Not bad." It is exactly like the one he's wearing. He shrugs and puts it on, then leaves.

Later in history class, Lucas rests his head on a book spread open on his desk. His eyes are closed. The class is discussing oil drilling and the environment, when a woman's voice comes over the loudspeaker. *"Lucas Reilly, you're wanted in the principal's office."* Lucas doesn't move. The other students look over at him. A few minutes pass. A shriller voice repeats over the loudspeaker, *"Lucas Reilly, you're wanted in Mr. Hayes office immediately!"* Still, Lucas doesn't budge.

A few more minutes pass. Finally one of Lucas's buddies, Gordy, leans over and punches Lucas in the arm, startling him awake. Lucas jumps up and shouts, "Oil drilling SUCKS!" then sits down. The class explodes in laughter.

Walking over to Lucas's desk, Mrs. Asher says, "Lucas, now that's two reasons for you to stand up quickly and head to principal Hayes's office right now."

Still dazed and looking through Mr. Hayes's rippled glass door, Lucas can see a man and a woman sitting across from the principal. "Ugh, my parents are here." He opens the door and walks in. At first he's relieved it's not his mom and dad, but then Lucas hears principal Hayes on the phone. "Yes, Mrs. Asher, I'll take care of that." Principal Hayes hangs up. "Lucas, this is Officer Morrow and Officer Davis from the Central police department. They have a few questions they'd like to ask you. Lucas, this is not an official interrogation or I'd call your parents in. It's just a few questions about your job."

Lucas takes a seat. He catches a glimpse of the female cop. She's his moms age and tough looking. Lucas notices her badge and her gun. Lucas starts to feel funny, nervous-like, and he can't stop looking at Officer Morrow's gun. The male officer has a gun too. Officer Morrow starts in right away.

Officer Morrow: "Lucas, do you work at the Morrison's crematorium."

Lucas: " I do."

Officer Morrow: "Yesterday, what time did you arrive at work?"

Lucas : "Around six."

Officer Morrow: "Do you have your own key?"

Lucas: "I have one, but we don't need keys, the back door is open to employees."

Officer Morrow: "Was anyone else working there?"

Lucas: "No, just me."

Officer Davis: "What is your job at the crematorium?"

Lucas: "I count the urns, check them in, polish them, and clean up any ashes on the floor."

Officer Davis looks over at officer Morrow with a bit of an eye roll.

Officer Morrow: "Did anything unusual occur yesterday?"

Lucas: "No, DEAD as usual." Lucas cracks himself up, but no one else finds it amusing. "Sorry, no."

Officer Morrow : "Lucas, what time did you lock up?"

Lucas is very tired all of a sudden and he's fighting the urge to throw up on principal Hayes's desk. He closes his eyes.

Officer Davis: "Hey, buddy, are you in there?"

Lucas opens his eyes. "Yeah, I'm here. I locked up at around seven and went home."

Officer Morrow: "Is there anything else you can tell us?"

Lucas thinks for a minute before he answers, closing his eyes again, the images of last night pop in and out. He can almost smell the strong odor of gasoline, but he's afraid that if he tells the officers what happened to him, they'll call his parents, and then his parents and the whole school will find out he works at the crematorium and he lied about his age. Or worse, the police will take him in for questioning, and then book him, and he'll miss playing against Hollbrook in the big football game on Saturday. Or worse yet, he'll lose his job for talking to the police, and whoever hit him on the head will come find him and finish the job.

Lucas: "No, there's nothing else."

Officer Davis: "You sure about that, kid? You know it's a criminal offense to withhold information."

Lucas: "Not that I recall." *I mean, it's not a lie if I say I don't remember something, right?*

Officer Morrow closes her report folder and thanks Lucas. She adds, "There was a small fire at Morrison's Crematorium last night. Someone called it in. Luckily, the fire department responded quickly, so there's only some minor water damage."

As Lucas listens, he realizes he should have told them

what happened. He feels nauseous. Officer Morrow and Officer Davis stand up, so Lucas stands up.

Officer Morrow hands Lucas a card, "If you can think of anything else, call me. The fire is under investigation and considered very suspicious."

Officer Davis gives Lucas the stink eye and puts his hand on his gun as he follows Officer Morrow out of the office. Lucas starts for the door.

Principal Hayes stops him, "Wait a minute, Lucas. That'll be one day of detention for that outburst to Mrs. Asher."

On his way out, under his breath, Lucas says, "Damn."

Mr. Hayes adds, "Lucas, that will be two more detentions. Have a nice day."

2

Mom, I'm Gonna Hurl

After school, still feeling queasy, Lucas skips football practice. As he crosses his street, he sees both of his parents' cars in the driveway. His sister Alex's car is parked on the street.

This is so not good. I'm in trouble. He decides to go around back. Webster, Alex's big scrappy rescue dog, trots around the yard and barks when he sees Lucas.

He whispers loudly, "Shush! Webster, quiet. Please."

Webster barks louder.

"Please be a good boy!" Lucas holds his finger up to his lips. "Shush!"

Webster keeps barking and runs circles around Lucas.

Lucas says, "Thanks, pal." The sarcasm oozing from his words. Lucas squeezes in through the screen door and gently pushes Webster away with his foot to keep him in the yard.

Once inside, Lucas runs up the back stairs. His mom

yells, "Lucas! Is that you?"

Lucas doesn't answer. He continues racing up the stairs, he's almost at his room when he runs smack into Gracie Feinberg, his sister's college roommate, who he's had a crush on since Alex brought her home a few months ago.

Lucas, now splayed out on the floor, stammers out an apology, "I'm... I'm so so-sorry, Gracie. I—"

"What the hell, dork." Alex interrupts him as she runs out of her room.

Still feeling queasy, Lucas jumps up, gags, then throws up on Gracie, who reacts by throwing up on the floor.

Alex shouts, "What's this? A freakin' barf-fest?"

Webster, meanwhile, has found his way into the house and to the second floor. He licks up what Gracie heaved on the floor. Alex gags at the sight. "Mom, come up here right now, or I'm gonna hurl."

Later, Lucas sits across from his parents on the sofa in the living room. His dad, Robert, is on his cell phone. He calmly holds the phone away from his ear to address his son. "Lucas, what's going on? The police and the school called, then your mother called me to come home from work."

Patricia chimes in. "Robert, please get off the phone." Robert puts his cell phone down. You can still hear the person on the other end talking. Robert lowers the volume. "It's work,

Patricia. It's important."

"So's your son, Robert," she adds. "Did you know that he works at the Morrison Crematorium where they burn up dead bodies for burials?" Trying to maintain her temper and shaking her head in disbelief, "What were you thinking, Lucas? You're only fourteen. Have you gone nuts?"

Robert adds, "Lucas, that place is a nightmare."

Lucas simply stares at them. Patricia squints her eyes to get a better look at him, then gets up and walks over to the couch. She's still wearing her hygienist uniform from Dr. Winston's dentist office, which makes her feel like she's a real doctor and gives her the right to make quick diagnoses. As she stands over him, she touches his forehead. "Are you sick? You feel warm. Robert, please go get the thermometer."

Lucas, annoyed, brushes her hand away. "No, Mom. I'm fine."

"Well, you look sick. Are you depressed? Anything you want to talk about? Something at school?"

"No, Mom." Lucas jumps off the couch. He towers over his mother. "I'm okay, Mom, I swear. I work at Morrison's for a couple of hours a week after school. It's always busy. It's a big business. I have nothing to do with the bodies." Lucas sees his mom grimace. He knows she's the nervous type. He's heard her over the phone talk about her anxiety with her three sisters, who are also "high strung." Unfortunately, Lucas feels like he's inherited his mom's anxious gene. He worries a lot about her and just about everything. He feels like his only safe way out is to downplay his interest in the job. "I'm safe, I'm fine, and I basically just clean up a little. You both said I needed to find a job after school. This was the only place that would hire me." Robert listens to Lucas and finds his explanation reasonable. He's also dealing with a bigger problem at work. He picks up his cell phone, the voice on the other end is still talking.

Robert stands up and pulls out his keys as he holds the phone away from his ear.

"I've got to get back to work." He walks over to Patty. "You've got this." He gives her a kiss on the cheek. "Robert, don't you have something to say to Lucas?"

As he walks out, he says, "Lucas, next time check with us before you take a job. Maybe find one that's a little less depressing." He walks out the door. "Yes, I totally agree," he says into the phone.

Lucas would love to tell his dad that he likes working with the dead, he feels calmer with them, but he's afraid his parents will send him to therapy like they did with his sister, Alex, when she started throwing up after every meal. "Mom, I've got homework." Lucas's number-one excuse. "Okay, Lucas, you can go, but this discussion is not over." "Yeah sure, Mom." Lucas bolts out of the room. All he can think about is that Gracie Feinberg, the girl of his dreams, is upstairs in his sister's bedroom right now.

At the same moment, upstairs in Alex's bedroom, Alex, 17, with sandy wavy short hair, tall and lanky like her brother, says to Gracie, "Ugh, my brother is such a loser."

Gracie, 16, has only met Lucas one other time, and she actually thought he was cute in an awkward, pathetic way when he smiled. Gracie is far from awkward or pathetic when she smiles. Gracie's small and pretty in an unusual way with hypnotic green, almond-shaped eyes, dark straight hair, and a practiced, confident, full lipped smile that shows two rows of perfect white teeth.

Both of her parents are doctors. Her mother, Akiko, born in Japan, studied at Harvard Medical School where she met Benjamin—Gracie's dad, straight out of Brooklyn, New York—in the Operating Room. Gracie mostly parented herself growing up and was probably stricter on herself than either of her parents. Their home was designed for efficiency not charm. Even Gracie's bedroom was sparse with no trace of Gracie's own choices or personality. As she looks around Alex's warm, sloppy, crowded, pink bedroom, she thinks. *This is exactly the room I wanted as a child.*

Smiling, Gracie remembers Alex's first words to her as they met in their dorm room. Looking straight at her, Alex said, "Wow, you're really pretty. Thank goodness, I'm really funny."

Alex then walked over to Gracie and gave her a giant hug. No one had ever told Gracie that she was pretty or hugged her with every ounce of their bony body. A bond was formed forever.

"Gracie is still smiling as she looks around the room. Alex asks, "What's so funny? It's Lucas, isn't it? Don't even think about being nice to him."

"No, Alex, it's not about Lucas. Gracie stops smiling and gets serious, "I'm just so bored with myself. I've always been such a good girl: good manners, good grades, you know I graduated high school early. I've been in an AP program all through high school. I worked my ass off. I missed all the normal fun. And for what? To be a stressed out doctor with no social life. I've never even been kissed or on a real date... I once got fixed up with one of my mother's friends' son...He was kinda cute but he was rude to our waiter, rude to the uber driver, rude in general and then he tried to kiss me. I was so depraved I considered kissing "rude boy" just to chalk it up to kissing someone other than my dad."

Gracie now has tears in her eyes. "Something in me is missing. I'm under-developed." Alex laughs and sits down next to her, "You're not under-developed Gracie, and what's that even mean? You're just experiencing yourself."
"As your appointed freshman mentor I'm supposed to help you navigate your first year here, well that's a joke but I can promise you, your life is going to get better with me around, I'm a blast."

At this point, Webster, the barfinator, jumps up on Alex's bed, circles, and plops down next to Alex, on all the mess, and continues to lick his whiskers and joyfully wag his tail.

Downstairs in the kitchen, Patricia sits at the kitchen table with Noreen, one of her three sisters, who came over immediately when Patricia texted her. They are drinking coffee.

"How about something sweet to go with this cold coffee," Noreen says, sort of laughing.

Patricia curtly remarks, "You're really asking me for a piece of cake right now? Just when I find out my son is working at a crematorium, where they burn dead bodies for burials, for none other than Matt Morrison, Fairfax's own original delinquent? This is not funny, Noreen."

Noreen replies with a smirk, "Patty, Matt Morrison was not that bad. He was in Barbara's grade in high school, he was cute, and I think she went out with him. You're totally overreacting. Nothing bad happened to Lucas. He just took a part-time job that's a bit creepy to make some extra money. Give the kid a break, will ya."

"Maybe you don't remember, Noreen, that one of the Morrisons family members was murdered in that mansion and supposedly the guy's ghost haunts the place."

Noreen can't contain her laughter. "Patty you really don't still believe that story, do you? We were kids when that happened, and as far as we know the guy died of natural causes."

Patty says, taking a sip of coffee and making a face, "Yeah, cause the guy knew where all the other Morrison family members were buried."

Noreen stands up and goes over and opens the refrigerator door, looks in, and pulls out some containers. She opens each one and smells them, checks the expiration dates, and puts them on the table. She grabs two forks from a drawer. As she digs into one of the containers she adds, "Lucas is a smart boy. He knows how to take care of himself. Stop worrying."

Patricia, disgruntled, stands up to make a new batch of coffee.

Noreen says sweetly, "Sis, while you're up, could you bring me some sliced turkey to go with this coleslaw?" Still eating out of the containers, Noreen adds, "Besides, Patty, we both know nothing bad ever happens in Fairfax."

3

Where's Waldo?

The next morning while walking to school, Lucas's cell phone buzzes. He takes out his ear buds and pulls the phone out of his back pocket. Gordy is on FaceTime. Behind Gordy, it's chaos: sirens are wailing, red lights are flashing, a camera crew is setting up, students are running around.

"Crap! Gordy, is there a shooter?" Before Gordy can answer, he gets bumped by a cameraman and his phone drops. "Gordy, you OK? Hey man, answer me. Gordy! Gordy answer me." Lucas takes off. As he gets closer to school, he sees a mob of police cars with red lights flashing, and hears principal Hayes on the loudspeaker.

"Students, there is no emergency. Please notify your parents. There is no event. Fairfax high school is not under attack! Please head straight into the auditorium."

Lucas finds Gordy. They fistbump and head into school with the rest of the students.

On the way inside the building, someone hands Lucas

a printed copy of the front page headlines of the local paper. There's a big class picture of Tucker Baron on the front page. The headline and accompanying article below the picture reads:

LOCAL FAIRFAX TEEN TUCKER BARON IS MISSING! An all out search is underway for the local teen. If you have any information, please contact the Central police station.

Lucas says to Gordy, "My mom will be all over this."

Once inside the auditorium, it takes principal Hayes a good ten minutes to quiet down the students, and that's only after he invites Captain Ward, head of the Central Marin police force, up to the podium. Captain Ward is a burly, no- nonsense, senior police officer, who's left a wake of local teens quaking in their shoes just hearing his name. He yells "ORDER!" from the podium. The auditorium goes silent.

"Listen up, this is serious business. Tucker Baron, your fellow classmate, is missing. His parents filed a missing persons report this morning. Tucker was last seen Wednesday night, October 26, around 6:30 p.m. in a blue Mustang. He never returned home Wednesday night. These kinds of disturbances don't happen in my jurisdiction, and my police officers need your help to carry out their job. The quicker we find your classmate, the better for his survival. Timing is everything in a missing persons case. If this is a hoax or a prank or any one of you is withholding information that might lead us to Tucker's whereabouts and you don't come forward now, I will personally throw the book at you and do everything in my power to get you sent away."

The auditorium breaks into loud chatter. Captain Ward blows a piercing whistle and the students go silent again. Captain Ward continues, "The police officers behind me—Officer Morrow, Officer Davis, Officer Cleeker, Officer Drew—please step up to the podium." Once they do, Captain Ward continues. "Some of these officers will be stationed in your school and will be interviewing students around the clock. They are here to help you help them to bring Tucker Baron home safely. Classes will continue on a regular schedule."

The whole auditorium makes one big "UGH!"

Later, at lunchtime, the Fairfax high school lunch hall is a madhouse. It sounds like a radioactive beehive with Drake's music in the background. Everyone wants to know where Tucker is.

Lucas is sitting at a lunch table with his buddy, Gordy, listening to some other kids at his table gossiping.

"I heard there's a ten million dollar reward for finding Tucker."

Another kid says, "My parents would pay ten million dollars to get me kidnapped." They all laugh nervously.

Lucas looks over at a lunch table across the room. It's a bunch of sophomores, the so- called popular crowd, only one grade up, but world's apart from Lucas and Gordy who are freshman. Tucker, the missing kid's seat is empty. He is part of that crowd.

Gordy, Lucas's friend since kindergarten, says, "Lucas, you could totally find Tucker. You love all this kinda stuff." Lucas is a bit nerdy. Actually he's just curious about things. Gordy has known Lucas forever. Lucas was brilliant at legos and anything he could find to take apart and put back together. Lately, Lucas and Gordy haven't played much of anything. Gordy's parents are newly divorced, so he has to go stay with his dad every other weekend in San Jose.

So naturally, Lucas and Gordy have drifted apart and are not as close. Gordy is leaving for his dad's place either today or tomorrow. At least Gordy misses some school.

But for now they are observing the older, popular table like they are watching Animal Planet. You can almost hear the English narrator describe the behavior of the male rhinoceros sizing up another male rhinoceros who's interested in the female rhinoceros sunbathing topless at the watering hole. Gordy and Lucas would never admit to each other that they are each somewhat interested in being popular now, but really, they are interested in being with girls. They are both clueless.

Lucas turns to Gordy after observing Brent Morrison, who appears to be the leader and who actually has a girlfriend, behaving with such confidence, and remarks. "What does Brent have that we don't?"

"How about money, a personality, and good looks for a starter."

Lucas, disheartened, is the kind of kid, who once wanted the video game "Call of Duty" for Christmas so badly it hurt. When he didn't get it, all he said was, "I never wanted that video game anyhow." Now he says to Gordy, "I could care less." He figured with that attitude he would never be disappointed. As they continue to watch the other table, Lucas wonders aloud, "So, where do you think Tucker is?"

Gordy takes a bite of his greasy pizza. "Don't know," he mumbles with a full mouth. "Why don't you figure that out. You like that detective stuff, and there's a fifty thousand dollar reward." The pizza grease rolls down his wrist.

Lucas says "What would you do with the reward money?" Gordy answers with his mouth full. "That's easy. I'd book a trip to Amsterdam. The girls there love American boys."

Lucas thinks for a minute and says. "All I want is a car... any car," as he looks over at the popular table he thinks to himself. *Only guys with cars get girls.*

At the other table, Brent continues laughing with his buddy Cole. Vicki, his girlfriend, sits far away from Brent. She is visibly upset as she polishes her nails while her friend, Mimi, holds a straw in a can of Diet Coke to Vicki's mouth, so she can keep polishing her nails without smearing them. Danny, another popular kid, who's laughing and eating, suddenly starts choking before spitting out something he was still eating. Once dislodged, the food lands on Brent's shirt. Brent stands up angrily.

Cole stands up too in reaction. "Dude, let it go." Brent thinks for a minute, then sits back down and smirks at Danny, "Hey, man, not funny."

Danny, understanding he just dodged a bullet, says, "Sorry, Brent."

Brent looks over at Vicki who's quietly crying.

Watching all this, Mimi picks up Vicki's nail polish and goes over to where Brent is sitting and "accidentally" on purpose spills some of the open RED nail polish bottle on Brent's shirt. Brent stands up and finally explodes. "Are you kidding me, Mimi?"

Vicki looks at Brent going off on Mimi and blurts out, "What if Tucker really is dead?"

The table goes silent. The whole lunchroom goes silent.

Cole answers, "Nah, Tucker's too cool to get messed up. He probably stole his dad's Amex and is on a beach in Cabo."

Everyone joins in at the same time. "Yeah, he's too cool."

Flashback:

Wednesday at 6:30 p.m. the night Tucker disappeared

Standing face to face, both obviously upset, Brent and Vicki are in a very heated argument in Brent's garage. Brent is waxing his snowboard. The garage is filled with tons of sporting equipment. Vicki is shivering and says, "Brent, I just don't understand you. How come you say you want to be with me, but you picked this weekend to go to Cole's stinky ski shack? You don't even know if there'll be enough snow, and you knew that it's Mimi's pre-Sweet Sixteen party."

Brent keeps waxing his snowboard and doesn't answer.

Hands on her hips, Vicki sniffles and says, "Brent, if you don't go to Mimi's with me, it means you don't care about me."

Brent still doesn't answer. He glares at Vicki. He can't understand why she doesn't get that she's his girl. She's been his girl since he first laid eyes on her in fourth grade. Vicki also knows that Brent hates being ordered around. He looks at the snowboard he's holding and says, "I'm going with Cole."

Vicki says, "Well then, I'm going now, and I'm not sure when I'll be back." Vicki picks up her backpack and says as she walks out the garage door, "You're making a big mistake."

Outside, she retrieves her cell phone and makes a call. "Meet me in fifteen minutes."

4

The Unnamed Urn

Back at the mortuary, after school, the day after Tucker's disappearance, Lucas uses an army roll call to check in the unclaimed urns to make the task a little less dreary. He breaks into a military commander's voice.

"Marianne Holtz?"

Lucas answers himself in a high women's voice. "Here!"

"Mr. William Ketchum," Lucas answers in a low bass voice. "Present!"

"And lastly, the honorable Benjamin Forman, Esquire." Then, in a goofy British accent, he says, "Here, Here!"

Lucas starts coughing from the still-smoky air from the fire. He goes to grab some water that he left on a shelf and notices an urn he's not seen before. He picks it up. There's no engraving on it, but it's heavy, which means it's full of ashes. He's holding the urn when the door opens and Scorch walks in. Scorch's real name is Toby Wallace, but everyone calls him Scorch because he works the cremation ovens. He's worked for the Morrisons for years. He takes his job very seriously and acts like the executioner from one of those old horror films he watched with his dad. Lucas thinks he must be blackmailing the Morrisons to keep his job for so long.

Scorch says he owns a house in town but mostly stays in one of the back rooms at the mortuary. Lucas doesn't think he has a wife or kids. He has a wicked sense of humor and a sinister laugh to match. There are terrible red scars on his face, and he wears thick coke bottle glasses, which make his eyes look magnified and frightening. Lucas would describe him as ghoulish looking, and he tries his best to stay clear of him.

"Hey, what you got there, buddy?" Scorch inquires.

Lucas answers, "Nothing but an old paint can."

Scorch squints to see. "Why are you acting so weird?"

Lucas starts fake coughing and turns around to hide the urn, while Scorch continues searching for something.

"All you boys are the same: jokers! Spoiled little jokers. I know you know that Morrison kid. I knew his dad growing up, and he was a troublemaker—like father like son. One day I'm going to teach all of you jokers a lesson you won't forget."

As Scorch continues rambling on, he gets himself worked up enough to start coughing uncontrollably. He reaches for an old coffee mug on a shelf and takes a sip and spits it out..

"It's poison, you kids are trying to kill me." He throws what's left in the cup on the wet debris from the fire. "That was some neat little fire we had here, could have burnt the whole place down." He's got a gleam in his eye that screams "pyromaniac." Scorch moves closer to Lucas, but Lucas backs away. Scorch smells like one hundred dead cigarette butts.

"So, listen, kid. I heard voices in here a few minutes ago. If I catch anyone else in here, you'll all be toast. No more funny stuff or I'll have you fired." He laughs and repeats, "I'll have you 'fired,' get it? 'Toast,' that's funny too."

Scorch leaves the room. Lucas picks up the unidentified urn and hides it. He's thinking. *Seriously, that urn filled with someone's ashes wasn't here last night. It's new, and it's still warm. Who's in there? Who put the cremation oven on and why? Something sketchy is definitely going on here.*

When Lucas gets home, Alex greets him at the door. She's holding his flannel shirt. Gracie is standing with her.

"Why is there blood on your shirt, Lucas? Did you kill Tucker? Or anyone else?"

The local paper is lying open on the sofa in the living room with Tucker's picture on the front page.

Lucas says, "Not funny, Alex," and grabs his shirt and runs upstairs.

Alex yells up the stairs. "You know, dimwit, Gracie is staying at our house for a few days. She's in pre-med, and she's taking a pysch criminology course, so if you did kill that show-off Tucker, she'll find out."

Lucas slams his door. Once inside his room and holding his bloodied shirt, the memory from the other night at the mortuary comes back again. The blood on his shirt must be from the hit he got on the back of his head. It's all still a bit foggy. He feels the back of his head, there's still a sore bump.

"I must have blacked out. I remember it was very hot. The cremation oven was on. And the new urn today. What was that all about?" He takes out Officer Morrow's card, and he flops on his bed. As he stares at the card and says out loud... "Yes, Officer Morrow, something unusual absolutely friggin' did happen."

There's a knock on Lucas's door. "Alex, go away!" Lucas shouts. The knocking continues. "Seriously, Alex, I'll call mom if you don't go away." *Knock knock.* "Alex, not only are you not funny, you're also just mean!" *Knock knock knock.* Furious, Lucas jumps up and flies to the door, ready to kill his sister. But when he opens his door...

Gracie Feinberg says, "Lucas, did you really kill Tucker Baron?"

5

House Of Pain

A flashlight shines a bright beam on a bold black carved-out wrought iron sign hung in an arc above the front entrance: "THE MORRISON CHAPEL AND CREMATORIUM BY THE BAY." It's nighttime and the silhouette of the Victorian mansion against the moonlight looks like the Disneyland Haunted House. Someone wearing a black hoodie and holding the flashlight, runs up the steps and uses a key to unlock the door. Inside, it's dark. The intruder heads to the back rooms like they are familiar with the place.

In the mortuary room, the intruder shines a shaky light on a large row of decorative caskets and crematorium urns. It's very spooky in the dark. The nervous intruder accidentally bumps into something and trips and lands head first into an open casket on display. A muffled "jeez'" fills the silent room. The lit flashlight falls to the floor and starts to roll. The floor creaks as the flashlight clanks along in what feels like slow motion... *rolling...rolling... rolling*, until there's a big "clunk" as it stops.

The intruder meanwhile is huffing and puffing, trying to climb out of the casket, as a fat hand with large red scars picks up the flashlight. Fumbling with it, the flashlight makes a ghastly light show flashing on the caskets and urns on display in the mortuary before finally landing upside down and shining directly into two huge bloodshot, watery eyes. It's Scorch. His voice bellows, "You're a dead man when I find you!"
The flashlight goes out.

Scorch makes his way to where the noise is coming from, and then -*THUD* -as a body goes down. It's dark, and you can't see who it is. There's a bit of light as someone runs out the door. The light shines on an urn on the floor next to a bunch of ashes.

Later that night, Lucas is in his bedroom on his computer. He's wearing a black hoodie, and a TV newsman is interviewing Principal Hayes in front of the school building. Mr. Hayes is holding his own microphone while the newsman continues to ask questions.
"Principal Hayes, are there any updates on the disappearance of high school student Tucker Baron? Any suspects in his alleged kidnapping or murder? Did he have any enemies?"

Mr. Hayes gets flustered. "Sir, no one has indicated that Tucker was kidnapped or any evidence of foul play. The central police force is fully committed to finding him. They will continue to conduct on-site interviews with his friends and the rest of the student body. We are all tirelessly working together to find Tucker and bring him home safely. Our community will never give up the search." Mr. Hayes's face is flushed, his blood pressure sky high, as he hands back the microphone.

There's a knock on Lucas's door. "Come in unless you're Alex." A voice on the other side of the door says, "It's Gracie Feinberg."

Lucas opens the door.

"Hi, Lucas."

"Hi, Gracie." Lucas's heart starts racing just seeing her again. He has no idea what to say to Gracie, so they watch the rest of the interview in silence.

Gracie says, "I know you didn't kill Tucker, but I'm obsessed with his disappearance. And actually, I have an assignment in my criminology class and Tucker's case is perfect for my paper. I mean I'd like to help find him. Since you live here and know everyone, maybe you could help me."

While Gracie is talking, Lucas is thinking. *Are you kidding? I'd help you find the Loch Ness monster.*

Meanwhile, Gracie is thinking while she looks at Lucas from the corner of her eye. *He's much cuter close up.*

Lucas, who's having trouble putting a sentence together, stammers, "The thing is, Gracie, now that I work in a crematorium and I'm with dead bodies all the time, I'm sure I could be of some assistance." As soon as he says "some assistance," he's mortified and turns back to his computer screen. *Who talks like that? I'm such a loser.*

Gracie just looks at Lucas and smiles. "OK, sure, Lucas, that's a big help."

Lucas wants to die. *Gracie is so out of my league.*

Flashback:
Wednesday at 6:45 p.m. the night Tucker disappeared

Tucker is driving his new blue Mustang, a sixteenth birthday present. He's driving alone around the neighborhood. Music blasts from his car. He drives down Main Street, then over to a park. He pulls over and waits. It's dark, so he puts his headlights on. A girl runs in front of the headlights. She opens the door and gets in. Tucker leans over and kisses her. She turns and faces him.

It's Vicki, Brent's girlfriend.

6

New Blue Mustang

On a back road outside of town, a police car turns off the road and pulls over to a car parked near some giant Redwood trees. It's a blue Mustang. The officers get out of their car. It's Officer Morrow and Officer Davis.

Officer Morrow says to Officer Davis, "What the hell is this kind of car doing abandoned on the side of the road? It looks brand new."

They both put on rubber gloves as they approach the obviously empty vehicle. It's unlocked. Officer Morrow opens the door, reaches in, and opens the glove compartment. She lifts out an envelope. She holds up the car registration and reads a name out loud: "Kyle Baron. That sounds very familiar." She thinks for a minute. "That's the guy who reported his son's car missing. So, this must be the car of the kid who is missing." She checks her notes. "Yup, a 2024 blue mustang with license plate 8VPZ6476. This is Tucker Baron's car." She hollers over to Officer Davis who's on the other side of the car. "Davis, put out an APB, call the station for backup, and get forensics over here now. This is Tucker Baron's car, and he could still be in the vicinity. This is now a crime scene." Morrow adds as Davis heads back to their patrol car, "Get the homicide squad over here too. We don't know what we're looking at."

Eager to find the missing teen, while Officer Davis calls in for backup, Officer Morrow walks around the front of the car and flips the lever to open the trunk. As she walks back to the trunk, she notices that a few feet from the car, there are fresh tire tracks and some torn up grass and mud. She takes out her notepad and jots down some notes and mumbles to herself, "...a second car...dug up tire tracks...fast getaway...possible accomplice." She gets to the trunk and looks in, half expecting to see a dead body in there. The moment is tense, she has a kid close to Tucker's age. She bends down to look deeper inside, and with half her body in the trunk, Officer Davis comes up right behind her.

"Morrow, need any help?" he shouts.

Startled, Officer Morrow jumps up quickly and wallops her head on the inside of the trunk's hood. Angrily, she says, "Jeez, Davis, no, you can not help me. You scared the friggin' soul right out of me!" She's still touching her head as a squadron of patrol cars with flashing red lights and wailing sirens close in on their location.

Police jump out of their patrol cars with walkie-talkies.

Forensics arrive, dressed in white, and in a flash are all over Tucker's car like seagulls devouring a bag of french fries left on the beach. Other officers quickly stretch yellow crime scene tape between the big Redwoods, fully securing the area.

Walking over to talk to the officers, Officer Morrow is a bit unsteady on her feet. She says to herself, "I swear I hear buzzing or ringing in my ears. Crap, I must have a concussion." The buzzing continues and even gets louder. She continues walking over to where the buzzing seems to be coming from. She bends down and sees a light in one of the grooves of the torn up tire tracks. She picks up a cell phone that's lit up and buzzing. She answers the phone.

A girl's voice says, "Tucker, are you alright?"

Morrow says, "Who's this?"

The phone goes dead.

Flashback:
Wednesday at 6:30 p.m. the night Tucker disappeared

Someone is walking around inside the crematorium. They are carrying a cardboard box. It's dark, except for a red glow from the EMERGENCY signs above the doors. You can only see the shadow of the figure. The shadow on the wall is big, bent over, and shuffling along. The figure puts the box down and reaches for a small shovel which is hung on the wall. The figure walks over to the oven, opens the big doors with a huge mitt also from the wall, and with the shovel, scoops up a pile of ashes. They then take out a strainer from the box, put the ashes into a strainer, and sift them like the old miners did looking for gold. Whatever is left in the strainer is transferred into a glass jar.

Right in the middle of the transfer, there's a loud noise from another room in the mortuary. Shaken, the figure closes the oven door with a bang, grabs a cremation urn from the unused urns on a shelf, and funnels the rest of the ashes into the urn. The figure places the jar and the urn back into the box with the other glass jars. When the figure places the box down to hang up the shovel, we can see what's in the glass jars: it's human teeth!

7

Shady Twins

The day after Tucker Baron's disappearance, it's business as usual at the Morrison Chapel and crematorium. Karen Morrison, a striking blonde, is talking to a Mr. Andrews, whose wife just died. He's holding a Kleenex box with "IF YOU CRIED WHEN A LOVE ONE DIED—Morrison's Chapel and Crematorium is right for you" printed on the side. Mr. Andrews is talking to Karen about how quickly his wife got sick and died. Karen listens sympathetically.

Mr. Andrews continues, "It happened so fast, she never knew what hit her."

Karen, a little slow on the uptake, responds, "Did they get the license?"

He looks confused. "What license?" Do I need a cremation license?"

The phone rings. Karen excuses herself and adds. "Don't worry, Mr. Andrew's, Mr. Morrison will be right out to help you make all the arrangements." She goes over to her desk, presses a button, and picks up the phone.

As if on cue, Jerry Morrison, with a once-handsome, now withered face, talking nonstop, comes out of a door in the wall that looks like a bookcase. "Hello, Mr. Andrews. I'm so sorry for your loss, and so sorry to hear about the accident."

Mr. Andrew says, "What accident? Who was in an accident?"

"Don't worry, we will straighten it all out and make all the arrangements. You're in the right place. We're here to help you."

Three new people walk in the front door. Karen motions for them to sit down. They squeeze onto a very old velvet lounge that must be from the turn of the century along with the rest of the furniture. Karen walks over and greets them, handing them a Kleenex box. "I'm so sorry for your loss. Someone will be right with you." She walks away and disappears into the same door that looks like a bookcase in the wall that Jerry magically came through.

Karen hears a man's voice booming from down a long hall. The voice gets louder as Karen gets closer to an office door.

Yelling, the man says, "Christ almighty, you're a friggin' idiot. A first-class nincompoop. How could you screw up a simple job like this? The place is made of kindling wood just waiting to go up. A friggin Boy Scout without a match could have finished the job. Wait! Now you're telling me someone else was there. Who was it? You hit him? Then you ran? Well, now you better make sure that someone never tells anyone. You friggin moron."

Karen walks into the office.

The man sitting at the desk on the phone has the same handsome, withered face as the man helping the mourners in the front parlor. It's Jerry's twin brother, Matt Morrison, who now says to the person on the other end of the phone, in a low, threatening whisper. "Listen, dummy, take care of him, or I'll take care of you!" Matt slams down the phone and looks at his wife and sweetly says to her, "What's for lunch?"

Karen smiles back at him and says, "Your favorite, pasta primavera. Jerry and I ordered takeout earlier. She goes around Matt's desk and gives him a kiss on his head. She walks out of the room.

In the hall she takes out her cell phone, makes a call, and says, "I can't talk now. I know, me too," and hangs up. When she comes out of the door in the wall into the front funeral parlor, Jerry is putting his cell phone into his pocket and holding down the contract on his desk that the three mourners are signing. He smiles at Karen and says to the mourners, "Please keep the gold pen, it's a gift from the Morrison Chapel and Crematorium by the Bay for taking the full Golden Cremation Package. We take care of everything, you just provide the loved one". The grieving woman starts to sob.

Later that night after dinner, Karen tells Matt she has to go get something in her car. She says she'll be right back. She doesn't know that Brent, her son, happens to be watching out of his bedroom window. Brent notices a car parked in front of his house. His mom stops at her car, grabs something, walks out to the parked car, and gets in. Brent turns away.

Flashback:

Wednesday at 7:00 p.m. the night Tucker disappeared

Brent plays a video game in his room when Cole knocks on his door. Without waiting, Cole barges into the room. Brent keeps playing while Cole makes wild gestures to get his attention. Finally, when Brent's guy goes down and the screen is spattered in blood, he throws off his earphones and says, "Cole, you better be here to tell me that there's a blizzard in Lake Tahoe and skiing is amazing."

Cole answers, "Well, I'm not sure about snow yet, but I am sure of what I saw five minutes ago." Brent, totally uninterested, starts to put his headphones back on when Cole quickly adds, "I saw Tucker driving his new blue mustang with Vicki, your girlfriend, in the front seat."

Brent throws his headphones across the room. He stands up and faces Cole."What did you say?"

Cole repeats himself.

Brent walks over to his weights and starts lifting them so fiercely that Cole instinctively backs away from him. Brent says sinisterly, "What a dirtbag. Tucker will pay for this."

Cole nods his head in agreement. "Yeah, what a dirtbag."

8

Webster Gets A Treat

It's been two days since his classmate Tucker went missing. Lucas is walking home on Main Street in Fairfax, after football practice. He notices some "missing person" posters for Tucker Baron on a few store windows. Distracted, Lucas almost sideswipes Bridget, a friend from school, who is trying to pull down the heavy closing gate in front of a thrift shop.

A bit shaken by the near collision, Bridget says, "Hey, Lucas, what's up? You almost knocked me down. You OK?"

"Sor-sorry, Bridget," he stammered. He doesn't want to admit that Tucker's posters have shaken him up. Lucas notices that his hands are sweating and his heart is beating faster. He takes a deep, loud breath through his nose. His anxiety doesn't go unnoticed by Bridget as he wipes his hands on his jeans and adds, "Did it cross your mind Bridget, that one of us could be next."

Bridget chortles a half laugh. "Lucas, that's if you believe Tucker was snatched. You know, like kidnapped."

When he hears "snatched," Lucas feels his face flush red. Not wanting to keep talking about Tucker, Lucas says, "Here, let me help you get that." He wipes his hands again on his shirt. As he reaches up to grab the gate, he winces in pain from the fall he took at practice earlier. Ignoring the pain, he jumps up and pulls down the gate and holds it down as Bridget secures the lock at the bottom.

"Thanks, Lucas." She picks up her bag on the ground and starts walking up the block. As he watches Bridget walk away, Lucas notices that Main Street is desolate. Most of the shops have closed for the night.

Bridget yells back at Lucas in a Darth Vader voice. "Lucas, go home. It's dark, and the kidnapper could be waiting for you in the bushes…with his lightsaber!" She laughs. They were both Star Wars fans together at one time. Lucas gives Bridget a nervous smile and sort of waves goodbye.

As Bridget waves back at Lucas, she notices a strange man, about thirty feet from where Lucas is standing. He's big, unshaven, in a cheap, shiny suit, which is too small for him, and has one hand in his pocket and a cigarette in the other. His suit jacket collar is up, like he doesn't want to be seen. He's looking into a shop that's closed. She says to herself as she locks in on his retro shiny, black, pointy dress shoes. "They would be great in the thrift shop." As she's checking out his shoes, she sees that the man keeps looking over at Lucas, and then looking away, which makes the guy look suspicious.

Is he stalking Lucas? Bridget thinks for a minute. *Nah, I'm just being paranoid.* She turns and walks toward home but speeds up her walk a bit.

As Lucas walks on, not only does his shoulder hurt, his leg starts to cramp. He has to stop from the pain. When he stops, the stranger down the street stops. Lucas limps into the deli. Sal, the owner, is sweeping up and getting ready to close.

"Hi, Sal," Lucas says as he puts some money on the counter.

"Hi, Lucas," Sal says.

Lucas grabs a gatorade in the back. He finishes the bottle in two gulps, releases a big burp, and says, "Thanks, Sal," then walks out.

Lucas walks further on Main Street, until there are no more stores, then crosses the street. He stops on the other side and looks back to where he was just standing, expecting to see Bridget still standing there. He has an eerie feeling he's being watched. As he continues walking home, the moon casts a faint and unreliable light as it's eclipsed by the tall pine trees lining the street and forming a tree tunnel above him. Ghostly shadows appear and disappear around him. As the wind picks up, he hears rustling behind him, but assures himself it's only his imagination as he walks over a bed of pine needles that cover the earthen floor.

It's dark. Lucas takes out his earbuds. All this darkness suddenly spooks him. It doesn't help that he can hear his mother's voice in his head. "Lucas, promise me you won't walk home alone, especially after football practice. There's a lunatic in the neighborhood." Now with every twitch of a breeze or rustle of a leaf, Lucas shudders. A dog somewhere starts barking. Lucas is definitely rattled.

He picks up his pace, but his leg cramp stops him from getting too far. He swears he hears footsteps behind him. He listens and just when a cloud covers the moon and there is no light, he hears the crunching of leaves right before a form separates itself from some bushes and jumps out at him.

Lucas shouts, "Hey, what are you doing?" But before he knows what's happening, the attacker, who's wearing a ski mask, grabs him and puts his arms around him in a bear hug and squeezes. Lucas winces from the shoulder pain and lets out some karate yell that helps him gather all of his strength. He breaks free from the hold and elbows the guy in the stomach, which has no effect whatsoever. Lucas puts his head down and tries to head-bump him and notices the black, shiny, pointy shoes the attacker is wearing.

More annoyed now, the attacker comes at Lucas with two rapid blows to his face and stomach. Lucas falls backward to the ground. The guy jumps on top of Lucas, like a professional wrestler who jumps from the top of the ropes, and pins Lucas down easily. The guy's face is just inches away from Lucas's.

From under the ski mask, the attacker asks ironically in a gravelly voice, "What do I think I'm doing?" He pulls out a shiny serrated knife. "I'm going to kill you."

The guy stinks of gasoline and smoke. Lucas panics and tries to push the guy off of him, but his shoulder has no strength. Lucas is breathing heavily and sweating and his body involuntarily starts to shake under the guy.

"Stop that, you idiot," the attacker mutters with frustration. Knowing the attacker is annoyed, Lucas shakes even more, then he turns the shakes into a wiggle.

"Stop friggin wiggling kid." Lucas keeps wiggling like he has the heebie-jeebies. Irritated, suddenly the attacker sits up, pulls up Lucas, who's still wiggling, to a sitting position, and punches him in the jaw. Lucas falls flat on his back, out cold.

"That's it. kid, take a little nap." The guy stands up. He's still holding the knife that glimmers threateningly when the moonlight hits it. The guy slowly squats next to Lucas's unconscious body, his knee bones cracking with each inch he lowers himself. He's not a young guy. Gasping for air under the thick mask, he pulls it half way off his face. His neck and bottom of his face are dripping in sweat.

He points the blade of the knife towards Lucas's chest, deciding on just the right spot. He slowly and gradually lowers the blade until it's just about an inch from Lucas's heart. As he raises the knife straight up to plunge it down, a big wind unleashes dried leaves and pine needles that rustle enough to make the attacker look up. With no warning, Webster, the barfinator, Alex's dog, leaps out of the bushes and onto the attacker. As the attacker falls back, the knife drops from his grip, narrowly missing Lucas's neck.

Webster clamps down on the guy's wrist like the jaws of a great white shark. The guy tries to throw Webster off of him by spinning him around like a whirling toy, but Webster's jaws hold tight. Round and round they go, and all the time the guy is screaming at Webster at the top of his lungs. "Let get, you friggin beast, let go!"

The ski mask partially comes down and his arm is dripping blood. Webster finally releases himself, and the force of the spinning causes the guy to go flying into the bushes. Webster runs into the bushes and bites the guy on his leg. Webster then proudly prances over to where Lucas is motionless on the ground and plops down in front of him and growls. The guy, bloody and hurt, walks out of the bushes and looks at Webster protecting Lucas. Webster snarls, while the guy fixes his suit and brushes off the leaves. "I'll get both of you sooner or later." Webster growls and makes a move toward the guy, who quickly takes off holding his bloodied wrist.

Later that night, looking in the bathroom mirror, Lucas is

shaken. His nose is bleeding, his jaw is black and blue, and his eye is swollen half shut. There's a knock at the door.

From the hallway, Gracie says, "Are you alright, Lucas. I saw you limp up the back stairs. Can I come in?"

Lucas hesitates, then thinking maybe she'll have pity on him, he unlocks the door.

"Christ, Lucas, "You look horrible."

Lucas says," Thanks, Gracie, I know."

"Who did this to you?" She grabs a washcloth and starts to gently clean off the blood under his nose. Gracie is tender and efficient. No girl has ever been this kind to him or this close. Her face is inches away from his. His lips are inches from hers. He smells her shampoo. He closes his eyes. He feels like he's being pulled by a magnet to her lips. He's never felt anything like this before. Gracie also feels the pull and closes her eyes. They are about to kiss when Lucas's nose starts bleeding again.

Gracie grabs the wash cloth and pinches Lucas's nose, and says, "Put your head back." He follows her orders. They both laugh. The romantic moment may be over, but something has happened between them. They look into each other's eyes for the first time and smile.

Gracie, still pinching Lucas's nose, says, "Stand up and follow me. He does, and Gracie awkwardly keeps pinching his nose as they walk into Lucas's bedroom. She walks with him over to his bed.

He says, "Thanks, Gracie, I'll take it from here." He replaces her hand and pinches his own nose. He lies down on his bed. Even in his weakened state, he's embarrassed when he looks around his room. There's a big LeBron James poster over his bed and a huge lego Starship that he built with Gordy on his desk and another Star Wars poster on his other wall.

Gracie looks around. Lucas's closet is open and it's filled with a row of different colored plaid flannel shirts. She smiles. It's just the kind of bedroom and clothes she expected Lucas to have. Lucas watches Gracie smile, but his heart drops. *She totally thinks I'm a nerd.* He shuts his eyes. His chances of getting anywhere with Gracie just vanished.

She turns back to him and sees his nose is still bleeding. "More pressure on your nose." She looks concerned. "Lucas, please tell me what's going on. If you don't, I'll call Alex in here...or worse, I'll call your mother." In a very soft voice, she calls, "Oh, Mrs. Reilly, come upstairs. Lucas needs you!" Gracie raises her voice a bit louder. "Oh, Mrs Reilly...!"

Lucas says, "OK, OK, just stop. I'll tell you, but I'm actually not sure what happened. Twice this week, someone tried to murder me."

"What? Why didn't you say anything to your parents, or even Alex and me?"

"I'm not sure why. I was afraid if I said anything, I'd get in trouble. You know, lose my job, go to jail for something. The police make me want to confess to something criminal, even if I didn't do anything."

Gracie sits down on his bed. "OK, Lucas, give me the details."

"So it actually started the night Tucker went missing."

Lucas describes in full detail getting hit in the head at the mortuary, finding a new unnamed urn filled with someone's ashes, being attacked by a maniac wearing a ski mask, with a huge knife and pointy, black, dress shoes. "Seriously, Gracie, this guy that attacked me is definitely involved in Tucker's disappearance. I'm convinced. We have to find him before he kills Tucker…and then finds me." Lucas gulp is audible.

Gracie reaches up and touches Lucas's swollen lips gently. She moves closer to Lucas on his bed and says "Lucas, I'm all in." Gracie thinks. *This is just what I needed.*

Gracie stands up and says in an officious manner, "The thing that stands out to me is the new urn with no name on it. Like, who's in there?"

Lucas, thinking out loud, says, "So, Tucker doesn't come home on Wednesday night, the same night I'm working at the mortuary. The crematory oven goes on, which is totally unusual and suspicious, and then the next day working at the mortuary, I find a new unnamed urn with fresh new ashes.

Gracie huffs in frustration. As the two of them take a moment to think, they stare at each other in concentrative silence. An epiphany suddenly hits them. They simultaneously shout, "It's Tucker! Of course it's Tucker Baron's ashes. Both say "UGH!" together.

Gracie says excitedly, "Let's go get him."

Lucas stares at Gracie, she's glowing with excitement, and he totally forgets what he was going to say. "I— I already tried to get the urn. I broke into the mortuary the other night, but the urn was knocked over, the ashes were spread across the floor. Someone else wants that urn and would probably kill for it."

Gracie says regrettably, "I could have taken the ashes over to the crime lab at school so we could analyze the ashes and find out who is in the urn for sure."

Lucas gets up from his bed and dramatically limps over to his desk drawer and holds up a plastic baggie.

"Lucas, are you nuts? You want to get high now."

Lucas says " No, these are the ashes from the unnamed urn. I grabbed some."

Gracie runs over to Lucas and hugs him. She then takes out her phone and texts someone. She turns to Lucas and says, "I have an idea. Moving towards the door, Gracie says, "Feel better. I'll see you in school tomorrow."

Lucas looks surprised. "My school?"

Gracie says, "You'll see. Just get better fast. We have a

date at USC's criminology lab tomorrow after dark." She walks out.

Lucas is almost in tears from pain, but he's grinning thinking about the near-kiss in the bathroom and the hug he got from Gracie on his own bed under LeBron James.

She also used the word "date."

9

The Master Of The Oven

Scorch is sleeping on a crappy bed in a back room in the Morrison mortuary. It's dark. There are gasoline cans on the floor near the door and lots of glass bottles on shelves on the wall. A bit like a lab. There are a few bottles of gin in varying levels of near-empty next to Scorch's bed. There is a denim jacket stuffed into a cubby on the wall. Scorch's broken eyeglasses are lying on the floor.

The phone rings at the Central police station. "Central police department, Officer Reeves speaking. How can I help you?"

A muffled, gravelly voice resonates on the other end. "I know who started the Morrison fire on Wednesday night. It was an employee who works for them. His name is Toby Wallace, and he's very dangerous. They call him Scorch because he likes to start fires." The phone goes dead.

Officer Reeves logs the call and its content, stands up,

and walks to the back of the station. "Hey, Morrow, wasn't your case the Morrison crematorium fire."

Morrow says, "Yup."

"I just got a tip for you." Reeves puts a piece of paper down on her desk. She's holding a plastic bag with the cell phone that she found near Tucker's car while simultaneously reading the cell phone readout on her desk. Behind her on the wall are a bunch of missing children posters with the children's photographs and one of a missing teen with a picture of Tucker Baron. There's also a bulletin board with Tucker's school picture and other possible suspects' pictures in what looks like the current criminal case the police are building for Tucker Baron's kidnapping or murder.

While reviewing Tucker's cell phone text readout data, Morrow says, "Looks like Tucker had a thing for this Vicki Hess, the same girl who forensics traced to the call to Tucker's phone that I answered at the crime scene. Brent Morrison was another caller that day, and now a person of interest. Let's go talk to both of them."

She also grabs and reads the paper Officer Reeves put on her desk. Standing up, Morrow calls over to Davis. "First the school, then let's pay a visit to Toby Wallace, who they call Scorch. Seriously, this job gets crazier every day."

Davis gathers his stuff. "Why do you think the missing kid and the Morrison fire are connected?"

Morrow answers, "Don't know, but we're going to find out."

Gracie is sitting at a lunch table at Fairfax High. She's wearing glasses and carrying a USC tote bag. She's posing as a USC college recruiter and talking to Vicki and Mimi. Vicki looks a mess. Gracie says, "How many of you have boyfriends?"

Vicki starts sniffing. Mimi puts her arm around her and says, "Vicki just got dumped."

Gracie says, "Tell me about it!" like she's been dumped a million times. Vicki doesn't respond, so Gracie says, "No, really. Tell me about it." The girls both look at Gracie suspiciously. Seeing their reaction, Gracie says, "I'm a sociology major, I'm gathering relationship demographic information on your age group to help pay my tuition. I'm getting paid to be a recruiter."

Vicki starts crying again.

Gracie adds, "You know you can trust me. I've been dumped a hundred times. I'm the queen of dumps."

Vicki suddenly blurts out the whole story. She's sobbing, and it's hard to understand what she's saying. Gracie, listening intently, starts taking notes.

"It all happened Wednesday night," Vicki says. "First, Brent and I had a big fight. Then Tucker picked me up and we were parked. And then this horrible man in a ski mask knocked on the window and made us get out. He tied up our hands. I thought he was going to kill us. Then he put Tucker in his car and drove off." Vicki is sobbing by now.

Gracie doesn't miss a beat with her questions. "Wait, then who's Brent?"

Vicki says, "My boyfriend."

"I thought you were parked with Tucker."

"I was."

"I'm confused," Gracie says.

Mimi adds, "Me too."

Gracie leans in, an intensity growing across her face. "Have you heard from Tucker? Did you get the license plate of the kidnapper? What kind of car did the kidnapper drive? What time did this happen? Which way did he head out? What was Tucker wearing?"

Vicki blurts out between sobs, "A blue denim jacket."

Gracie continues her barrage of questions. "Would you recognize the man?"

"No, like I said, he had on a ski mask," Vicki says. "But... he smelled like smoke and gasoline. Oh, and he was wearing black, shiny, pointy shoes like he was going out somewhere special. It was odd."

"Did you tell the police?"

Vicki starts sobbing even harder. "No, I couldn't. The man said he'd kill Tucker if I told anyone. Besides, if my jealous boyfriend, Brent, found out about Tucker and me, he'd probably kill us both. He's way jealous."

"What's his name again?"

"Brent Morrison. But don't tell anyone."

As Gracie writes Brent's name in her notes, she sees two police officers walk into the lunch room. They ask a student to point out Vicki Hess. As they head toward Vicki, Gracie quickly says, "So sorry, I've got to run." She hugs Vicki. "You'll be all right. Both of those boys are losers. Dump them, work on your GPA, and apply to lots of colleges. Then you'll have plenty of choices in schools and college boys."

On her way out, she sees Lucas coming toward her with a friend. It's Gordy.

Gordy stares at Gracie and says under his breath, "Now that's my type."

Gracie walks over to Lucas and whispers in his ear, "Meet me in an hour at your house."

Gordy is in such shock, he trips and falls onto a table. Lucas flashes him a big grin.

Later in the lunchroom, Officer Morrow and Officer Davis sit at a lunch table questioning Brent Morrison, who's sitting with his buddy Cole. They finished with Vicki Hess earlier. She cried throughout the interrogation, still too upset to tell them anything. They will have to bring her into the station for questioning later.

Brent appears very twitchy. He can't sit still. His eyes dart around to see who's watching him. Office Morrow asks, "How do you feel about your good friend's disappearance?"

Brent answers rudely, "He's not my friend. Honestly, I can't stand him."

Officer Davis gives Officer Morrow a raised eyebrow, then continues. "You two have a fight or something?"

Brent says, "Tucker is a jerk and a dirtbag."

Cole nods his head in agreement.

Officer Davis continues, "Brent, where were you last Wednesday night?

Brent answers angrily, "I was home."

Cole adds, "I was with him all night."

Officer Davis nods. "Well, we will just see about that."

With Officer Davis's last remark, Brent stands up so hurriedly that he knocks over the chair he was sitting on. "Listen, officers. I don't have to answer any more questions. I have my rights. So if you're finished, I have to get to class."

Officer Morrow remarks as Brent runs off, "Well, Davis, we just got ourselves a new suspect."

Outside, at the same time, Gracie rushes down the front steps of Fairfax High. When she hits the sidewalk, she takes off at full speed toward Alex's house. Parked right near the school, she notices two police cars. She feels self-conscious, maybe because she just used a disguise to elicit information about

Tucker's disappearance.

As she walks swiftly away, she says aloud to herself, "I'm acting nuts. That police car probably belongs to the two police officers who walked into the lunchroom when I left, and the other one is probably always there. But what if Vicki is telling those two officers right now about me asking all those questions about Tucker. Maybe the police will come looking for me while I'm still near the school. I wonder if it's against the law to impersonate another person and a college recruiter?"

As she continues walking, she also notices a car going very slowly a few blocks away from her. The car looks familiar. She stops to think for a minute. *I've seen that car recently. I know, this morning that car was parked across the street from the Reilly's house. He must have seen me talking outside with Lucas.* The car is gaining on her. She picks up her pace and tells herself. *It's OK. How could he know what I found out?* But she suddenly notices the car is keeping pace with her.

To test her theory of being followed, she makes a quick right turn onto another street. Luckily there are kids playing outside in their yard. She sighs with relief and keeps walking when suddenly she sees the front end of the same car turning the corner and facing her. She says out loud, "Coincidence? I don't think so."

Her fear of being followed is confirmed. She starts to run, and the car starts racing toward her. She keeps running but realizes she can't outrun the car. When she turns around to see how close the car is, she stumbles and falls. The car stops at the curb right next to her. The motor stops.

The door on the driver's side opens. A sharp smell of smoke and gasoline permeates the air when the door opens. Just as a black, shiny, pointy shoe steps out of the car, a police car comes down the street toward her. Quickly, the foot slips back into the car, and the man speeds off, passing the police car on his way up the street.

She throws up her hands and flags down the police car. She's totally out of breath and stays down on the pavement.

Two police officers get out. "Are you all right?"

Gracie, breathless, takes a moment before she can answer. "Yes, just winded."

"Do you need an ambulance?"

"No, sir. I'm OK."

One of the officers says, "Here, let us help you up. Do you live around here?"

"Actually, no, I'm staying with my college roommate's family."

"Can you walk?"

"Yup." She's anxious just to get away from the police, but she's still unsteady on her feet, more from fear than from running.

"Why don't we drive you home."

Gracie doesn't reply. She needs a minute to think about what to do. *What if they ask me a lot of questions, and I get nervous and tell them about Lucas and the kidnapper? They could take me directly to the police station for more questioning.* She sits there like a deer in the headlights.

"You OK there, miss?" the officer in the passenger seat asks.

"I'm OK." She gives them the Reillys' address.

The police car pulls up to the Reillys' house. The officers and Gracie get out of the car and walk up to the front door and ring the bell. Patricia answers in her hygienist uniform. When she opens the door and sees Gracie between the two police officers, she's obviously upset. Gracie's pale.

Patricia grabs her and hugs her. "Gracie, what happened? Are you OK?" Patricia knows the two officers. "Lou, Al, come in."

Gracie says, "No need to worry, Mrs. Reilly, I'm fine. I took a run and I guess I was too ambitious and ran too far, and then I got lost." Gracie turns to go upstairs. "Thank you, officers. I'm really OK."

Patricia hugs Gracie again and says she'll come up and see her in a bit. Patricia then offers the officers, who are old high school buddies, some coffee and pie. The three of them head into the kitchen. Gracie can hear Patricia ask them for any news on Tucker's disappearance.

Gracie runs upstairs and knocks on Lucas's door. No answer. She can't wait to tell him what's just happened. As she heads into the bathroom for a shower, she's still shaking.

Flashback:
Wednesday at 7:30 p.m. the night Tucker disappeared

A blue Mustang is parked by the side of the road near the redwoods. The windows are fogged up. Inside, Tucker and Vicki are talking. Out of nowhere, there's a knock on the window. They both scream.

A gravelly voice says, "Get out of the car and don't turn around."

They get out and Vicki screams again when she turns around and sees the big guy wearing a ski mask.

"Quiet there, girly. You stay cool, and I'll stay cool."

He ties Tucker's hands around his back, then he ties up Vicki's hands behind her back. Vicki's crying.

Tucker says, "I'll give you any money you want. My dad is rich."

"Shut up, kid, and get in your trunk. To Vicki he says, "Go sit by the trees and keep quiet." He briskly walks away after he puts Tucker in Tucker's own car trunk.

Vicki tries to untie her hands. Tucker keeps yelling for

help from inside his trunk. In minutes, the guy comes zooming back in his car. He unlocks Tucker's trunk, blindfolds Tucker, and forces him into his car. The guy yells to Vicki, "If you say anything to anyone, this kid is dead. Got it?"

She nods her head.

He speeds off, leaving Vicki crying on a tree stump. In the car there's a serrated knife on the seat next to the driver.

10

Good Day, Sir

Following up the arson tip, Officer Morrow and Officer Davis now stand at the front door of the Morrison's Chapel and Crematorium by the Bay's mansion. When Officer Morrow tries the door, it's open. As they step into the front parlor, funeral organ music starts playing. The morose music stops when they step off the worn, faded floral area rug that covers the overly polished floor. The room resembles a Victorian funeral parlor with an ornate crystal chandelier that twinkles and makes fairy-like tinkling sounds. Dark green velvet lounges, gold-rimmed burgundy velvet chairs, and elaborate turn-of-the-century Tiffany table lamps that cast eerie shadows onto the dark mahogany-paneled wall, make up the interior. The funeral parlor appears to be empty.

Officer Morrow says, "Hello, it's the Central police department. Is anyone here?"

Looking for someone to help them, they head into an adjoining room. It's filled with all different kinds of burial caskets in all shapes, styles and types of wood. Each casket is lined in beautiful shades of pink and purple satin and white silk. Flowers flood the room and give off an overwhelming sweetly sickening aroma. Officer Davis notices as they leave the room that there's an air freshener dispenser on the wall that whooshes every time it disperses more floral fragrances.

"Hello, anyone here?" Officer Morrow says again. They keep walking and end up in another room, which is lined with shelves covered in velvet that hold highly polished cremation urns. Some are gold or silver, big and small. Officer Davis is getting more and more creeped out. They enter the chapel off of the urn showcase room. The dark purple and gold room is very empty. They walk out and see a sign on two closed doors that says "CREMATORIUM" and under it reads "NO ADMITTANCE."

Officer Davis says, "No way am I going in there anyway."

They head back to the entrance.

Suddenly as they step into the casket room, a man comes out of nowhere and says, "Can I help you?"

Davis jumps back and knocks over a table with a vase that crashes to the floor. Officer Morrow steps up. "Sorry about that. I'm Officer Morrow and this is Officer Davis. We're here from the Central police department. We got a call about a possible arsonist starting the fire here on Wednesday night. Apparently, he's one of your employees."

With a big phony smile…"I'm the funeral director, Mathew

Morrison." He tries to maintain himself, but he goes a little tight around his mouth. When he shakes Officer Morrow's hand, she notices it's sweaty.

Morrow adds, "We're looking for a Mr. Toby Wallace." Obviously relieved, Morrison says, "You mean Scorch. Yes, he works for us. I'm so sorry, but he's not here. He took a few days off to visit a relative. Besides, we worked with the Central fire department and the police. I thought it was determined that the case was closed. Please check with Captain James of the Central fire department if you have any more questions." As Mr. Morrison talks to the officers, he walks in the direction of the front door. "Let me walk you out, officers."

Officer Morrow stops in her tracks. "One minute. I have a few more questions, Mr. Morrison. Do you know where Mr. Wallace was on Wednesday night? Was he at work here? Does he have any family we can contact? Close relatives?"

Still trying to usher the officers toward the front door, Mr. Morrison says, "Sorry, officers, those are questions Mr. Wallace will have to answer for himself."

Finally at the front door, Mr. Morrison says hurriedly, "Well, officers, I hope I've helped your investigation. Have a great day." He quickly closes the door, the officers' puzzled faces disappearing behind it.

As Matt turns away from the door and steps on the rug, funeral music fills the room. Matt walks far enough away from the entrance so he won't be heard by the police, takes out his phone, and sinisterly whispers into it. "Scorch, come to my office immediately. And don't talk to anyone, especially the police."

Outside on the porch, Officer Morrow says, "That's one nervous dude, and I'm not buying that this Scorch guy is out of town. We'll come back after hours tonight with a search warrant. Something is shady with this guy's whole setup."

Gracie meets Lucas outside his house as planned. She runs up to him all nervous and excited. "Lucas, I was almost kidnapped today."

"Damn," Lucas says.

She tells him about the car following her, and she's sure that it was the kidnapper and that he knows who they are and what they are up to. "And then the police arrived just in time before he grabbed me, and then the guy drove off. Lucas, I understand how you felt about not telling the police what we're doing about finding Tucker on our own." She seems to tell him all this in one breath while she's getting into the driver's seat of Alex's car.

Lucas says, "Gracie, slow down. First of all, how did you get Alex's car keys without letting her know what we're doing?"

Gracie laughs, "Let's just say I 'borrowed them.' I'll tell her I had to go back to my dorm to get something, which isn't a lie."

"So if it was the kidnapper in the car following you," Lucas muses, "then he knows we are on to him. Gracie, this is getting serious. Both of our lives are in danger. Maybe we are in over our heads."

They both get very quiet as they drive along. Lucas looks over at Gracie and thinks, *I'm not ready to give up on finding Tucker or stop hanging out with Gracie.*

Gracie looks over at Lucas. *Maybe Lucas is right, but I'd hate not to see him and especially not finish what we started.*

"Lucas, I think it's too late to walk away now, I feel like we have no choice but to continue to find Tucker, and besides, I think we're a great team."

While Gracie is talking, all Lucas hears is the last part of what she said: we're a great team. Lucas feels overwhelmed, and his hands start sweating. He's never teamed up with a girl before, so right now with sweaty hands, he's nervously twirling the plastic baggie of ashes around and around in little circles above his lap.

Gracie notices and says, "Lucas, please stop twirling those ashes. That could be Tucker in there."

Lucas laughs nervously and stuffs the ashes in his jacket pocket. "Did you know, Gracie, that it's illegal to spread ashes in streams, rivers, and lakes, but it's OK in the ocean, the air, parks, and sports stadiums?"

"Lucas, seriously, what is wrong with you? Why do you want to know all that stuff about dead people?"

Lucas smirks, "I want to be prepared."

Gracie looks at him. "You really are dark."

He feels for the ashes in his jacket pocket again. *Maybe I am depressed.*

About an hour later, they arrive on campus. Gracie parks in front of the science building. A security guard is standing in front of the entrance. He's very serious and big. Lucas gets that funny-nervous feeling like he's guilty of something.

Inside, Gracie asks another student where the science labs are. They head up to the second floor. On the science lab door room 220, there's a "NO ADMITTANCE" sign. They go in anyway. No lights. It's a typical science lab like in high school filled with test tubes, Bunsen burners, glass tubes, glass jars, testing equipment, and in the back through a glass sliding door are cages with mice, a few rabbits, and an overweight hamster.

Gracie, disappointed, says, "I know there's a crime lab on campus with all the good crime-fighting stuff. You know, like equipment to test blood samples, DNA forensic stuff, firearm IDs, toxicology, and hopefully human remains analysis, like on CSI, that's why I signed up for the course."

Lucas laughs, "Who's dark now?"

Gracie laughs and gets an idea. She goes into her bag

and takes out her class schedule. When she finds what she's looking for, she gets excited. "Follow me. The crime lab we want is next door."

An identical "NO ADMITTANCE" sign is on the crime lab door. Lights are also out. The room is dark and small. There are a few machines that are unplugged and lifeless.

Gracie says, "So much for a misleading course description. They promised we'd all walk out of the course with enough criminal knowledge to join the FBI. I couldn't even join the girl scouts."

Lucas laughs and walks into the lab. He immediately trips on something and falls down. The baggie with the ashes falls out of his jacket. He scrambles on the floor like a snake to grab it. Gracie trips over Lucas's feet and falls on top of him. He wiggles along with Gracie on his back and grabs the baggie that's come untied, and then starts to sheepishly crawl out from under her. Startled by a noise at the closed door, both of their heads turn to the front as they watch the door handle start to move. They can see the shadow of the big security guy through the door. The handle fully turns and the security guy walks in with a flashlight.

"Who's in here? I know you're in here. You're trespassing. This is school property, so you're breaking the law. I've already called the police, so come out and show your face or go to jail."

Lucas, trying to protect Gracie, who's still halfway on top

of him, whispers to her, "I'll distract the guy, you run out."

Gracie whispers, "No way," but before she can stop him, he pushes her off of him and stands up.

"Sorry, sir. I'm a student, and I left my notes from class here. Luckily I found them, so good day, sir." Lucas tries to casually walk out the door.

The guy unexpectedly leaps out at Lucas, who's holding the open baggie of ashes in his hand. When the guy goes to grab him, Lucas throws the ashes in the guys' face and runs out the door with Gracie trailing behind him. They both fly down the stairs and into Alex's car, then race off. The police sirens are screaming in the distance.

Driving home, Gracie is hysterically laughing as she loudly mimics Lucas, but in a British accent. "'So, good day, sir.' Who are you? Oliver Twist?"

Lucas sort of laughs but can't believe he said that. He also has Tucker's ashes all over his jacket. He's thinking, *I'm so not cool.*

After the ashes incident in the crime lab, all Gracie wants to do is lie down when they get back to Lucas's house. She opens Alex's bedroom door and finds her standing there with her hands out. "The car keys, please, Gracie."

Gracie fishes around in her bag and pulls out the keys that are covered in ashes and hands them to Alex. "Sorry, I can explain."

Alex says, "No need," and saunters to her bed. Alex says in a scary stern voice, "Take a seat, Gracie." She pats on the bed where she wants Gracie to sit. "I have one question for you. Be honest. I'll still be your roommate and best friend. Are you sneaking around with my baby brother?"

Gracie almost falls off the bed laughing. "No, Alex, I thought you were going to ask me if I borrowed your Barbie pink cashmere sweater, which I did."

Alex sighs with relief. "Then what the hell is going on?"

Gracie zips up her lips. "I can't tell you."

Alex replies, "Then I'll tell my mother you're in love with Lucas."

Gracie thinks for a minute. "Sit down, Alex, cause you won't believe this." Gracie blurts out the whole saga about Lucas and her trying to find Tucker on their own. "I went undercover as a college recruiter at Fairfax high to get information from his friends about Tucker's disappearance. Then walking home I almost got kidnapped, but two police officers, who your mother knows, saved me and brought me here. I got stuff from Brent's girlfriend, Vicki Hessi, that the police don't even know. Tucker was kidnapped by a big thug, the same guy who tried to grab me, and Tucker may have been cremated. Actually the keys you're holding are covered in Tucker's ashes—we think."

Alex screams and throws the keys out the window. As she

keeps screaming, Gracie quickly covers her mouth.

"Alex, promise me you'll calm down if I take my hand away."

Alex nods yes, so Gracie pulls her hand away.

A wry smile is sitting on Alex's face. "I won't tell as long as you take me with you and Lucas next time. This is so rad!" They shake hands on it and then hug.

Gracie adds," I have to admit, Alex, Lucas is kinda cute."

"Ewww," Alex cries out.

11

Who's Jealous?

After dealing with Alex earlier in the other room, now Gracie sits on Lucas's bed in his room. Gracie is happily finishing up reading her notes to Lucas from her successful questioning of Vicki in the lunchroom earlier.

"Vicki was in Tucker's car, and this older guy wearing a ski mask knocked on the car window, made them get out, tied their hands behind them, made Vicki sit on a tree stump, put Tucker in Tucker's car trunk, then the masked guy left. When he came back with his own car, he transferred Tucker into his car and zoomed off, leaving Vicki tied up at the roadside." Gracie adds, "It must have been so scary."

Lucas agrees with a nod. "Did she go to the police?"

"No, she said her boyfriend would kill both of them if he knew she was with Tucker." Gracie looks at her notes. "Vicki's boyfriend's name is Brent Morrison."

"I know," Lucas says. "He's actually the son of one of the Morrison brothers—my bosses at the mortuary—and a big jerk."

Gracie takes out her criminology textbook and opens it. "Let's see what the book says to do with criminals." She flips back and forth until she finds the page and reads aloud. "Here we are. 'The elements of a crime are the criminal act, the criminal intent, concurrence, causation, harm, and attendant circumstances.'" She looks at Lucas. "I could never be a criminal. How could I be one if I don't understand how to be one." Gracie cracks herself up.

Lucas joins in her laughter, then adds, "Can I see that? It also says that 'criminals usually lack self control, can be impulsive, insensitive, risk-takers—'"

"That's my entire freshman girls dorm," Gracie interjects. "So let's see, who lacks self-control, is self-centered, bad-tempered, and has a real motive. Brent's jealous of Tucker." Gracie adds,"You know, Lucas, love can make you do crazy things."

Lucas replies, "Yeah, sure." He blushes a bit.

Gracie continues, "So, Brent Morrison checks all those boxes; he's our number-one suspect. He should be arrested immediately for the kidnapping and possible homicide of Tucker Baron. Done! Case closed!" Gracie stands up ready to leave the room.

"Gracie, wait," Lucas says. "Brent couldn't have kidnapped Tucker. Vicki said it was a big older man wearing a ski mask who smelled like smoke and gasoline. Lucas stops talking suddenly. "Gracie, the guy who tried to murder me also smelled like gasoline and smoke, actually just like the crematorium where I work."

"So the same man that attacked you on your way home the other night also kidnapped Tucker. Lucas, you really are lucky to be alive."

"And it wasn't Brent, for sure, who attacked me or Tucker."

"So where does Brent fit in?"

Lucas thinks for a second. "Gracie, Brent may have had an accomplice. Scorch once said that Brent is a bad kid like his dad used to be. Scorch knows a lot about the whole Morrison family. Maybe he knows how Brent is connected to all this. Let's go talk to him. He sort of likes me."

Gracie laughs. "That's a good thing? Lucas, since he likes you, you go see him and have a nice little chat. I'll stay here and think."

Lucas smiles. "Gracie, you're not afraid to meet Scorch, are you?"

Gracie laughs nervously, "No, not at all."

Lucas grabs Gracie's hand and gently pushes her out of his room. "Once we get there, I can introduce you to my buddies in the mortuary storage room."

Gracie shakes her head. "You really are a demented nerd."

12

You Have The Right To Remain Silent...

On their way to talk to Scorch, Gracie and Lucas drive around the back of Morrison's Chapel and Crematorium. In the moonlight, Morrisons Mortuary looks totally frightful.

Gracie says, "Lucas, no way I'm going in there. I feel like we're in a slasher film. Just… nope, no way."

"OK, you stay here, and I'll go alone."

"Seriously, Lucas, that's the exact dialogue that the boy says to the girl in every slasher film. Then two minutes later we hear the girl screaming, and when the boy gets back to the car, he finds the girl's guts spilled all over the front seat! No way I'm staying out here alone. I'll come in."

"Stay close to me, Gracie, I know the way." Lucas grins. He's no dummy.

At about the same time, a police car drives up to the front of Morrison's. The place is dark. Officer Morrow and Officer Davis exit their vehicle. They go up the front stairs and jimmy the locked door open.

Officer Davis says, "Spooky, right?"

Morrow uses a flashlight once they're inside.

In the back rooms, Lucas is also using a flashlight. Gracie is hanging on to Lucas's jacket as if they were one person walking. Lucas stops at the Mortuary Storage room door. Once inside, he flashes his flashlight on the unclaimed urns. When he sees all three are still there, he walks over to them.

"Hi, buddies." He's actually really happy to see them.

Before he can introduce Gracie, there's a loud crash in another room. Gracie screams and pulls on Lucas's jacket so hard it comes off. Running with Lucas's jacket in the dark, she trips and falls. Lucas runs after her.

Lucas helps Gracie off the floor. She hugs Lucas around the neck. He feels lightheaded from being so close to her. Regaining control of his senses, Lucas says, "It's OK, I know my way around the mortuary."

Gracie laughs, "That will be great on your college application. Lucas, you can put me down now."

Lucas puts her down. "Scorch's room is right around the corner. Let's at least check it out."

She grabs Lucas's hand, and he leads her to a room with a closed door. When she sees the closed door, Gracie pulls her hand away, and whispers, "I'm not going in there."

Lucas says, "OK, then just stand right here and be my lookout."

"No way," Gracie complains, but Lucas leaves her and goes in.

It's dark, and he hears loud growling noises. He sees Scorch sleeping on a bed in the corner, snoring loudly. The room reeks of gasoline and smoke. He walks silently around the room, then accidentally trips on something and falls with a-*THUD*. Scorch moans and moves a bit before sitting up. Lucas is right in front of him on the floor. Scorch looks around, but can't see anyone, so he lies back down.

Lucas knows Scorch is capable of hurting him and Gracie, so he's extra careful. Sweating, Lucas stands up and continues to look around. He sees a few cardboard boxes and opens one. There are about half a dozen glass jars. He holds one up. When he sees what's in it, he almost drops it. He has to hold his hand over his mouth to keep from reacting. He puts the jar back in the box and runs out.

He grabs Gracie's hand and whispers, "Wait till I tell you what I found." Lucas looks very pale. On the way out, Lucas, trying to be cool, quickly shows Gracie some secret doors hidden in the walls. One door leads to the upstairs, another door leads to the front funeral parlor, and one door leads into the crematorium. "Ugh," she says after he mentions the crematorium.

"What? Some of the most interesting people come from in there!"

While Lucas and Gracie rush to leave the mortuary, Officer Morrow and Officer Davis are making their way to the back where they think they heard a scream. When Lucas and Gracie hear footsteps, Gracie almost pulls Lucas down again. Luckily for them, the officers use a different hallway to get to the back, but the officers hear the footsteps too. Morrow pulls out her gun and whispers to Davis, "Someone else is here. Call the station for backup."

Officer Davis nervously walks away to call for backup. When he finishes, he quickly joins Morrow. It's hot and dark in the hallways. Davis is jumpier than usual. Morrow knocks on the first door they see, which creaks open by itself. Morrow motions for Davis to stay back as she goes in. After what feels like an hour, Morrow comes out and whispers, "Nothing but mortuary equipment."

Davis rolls his eyes and wipes the sweat off his face.

As they continue on, they both stop when they hear strange sounds coming from behind another door ahead of them. The noise is getting louder as they approach. It sounds like some kind of growling animal. A big animal. Sweat is pouring out of Davis. Morrow signals to Davis to move together to push open the door and enter. Morrow shouts, "Central

Police! Put your hands up!"

Scorch, still sleeping, gets so scared by the shouting waking him, he falls out of bed. He grabs for his glasses, but they're not on the table next to him. He can't see, so he doesn't know what's going on. Davis shines his flashlight on him. He's blinded by the light and yells, "Hey, stop that! You friggin kids! I thought I heard you kids in here before."

Morrow switches the overhead light on. There are gasoline cans near the door and the room reeks of gasoline and some kind of smoky smell.

Scorch stands up wearing his broken glasses. He can't see who's there. "I'm telling you kids you're all going to be barbecue meat when I get you!"

After noticing the gasoline cans and the alarming look of the room Officer Morrow motions for Davis to grab Scorch while he can. Davis reaches for Scorch, handcuffs him and says, "Toby Wallace, you are under arrest for the act of arson of the Morrison Chapel and Crematorium.

Scorch cuts Davis off, "What the hell are you talking about. I work and sometimes sleep here. I'm the crematorium oven master. What are you doing?"

Davis keeps talking. "You have the right to remain silent..." While Davis finishes up with Scorch, Officer Morrow notices a denim jacket stuffed in a cubby near the bed. She puts on her rubber gloves and pulls the jacket out. It has blood stains on it. She puts it in a plastic bag and walks over to Davis.

"The missing kid was wearing this kinda jacket when he disappeared. I'm thinking we've got a possible arson and maybe a kidnapper right here." On her way out, she almost trips on a cardboard box. She opens it. She pulls out a glass jar and gasps.

"Davis, wait until you see Scorch's unique collection here." She holds up a glass jar filled with human teeth.

Davis says, "Let's go, Toby. You have a date with us at the lovely Central Police Station, or should we make a quick stop at our friendly neighborhood dentist, Dr. Watson, to check out who's teeth these all might belong to?"

Police sirens wail outside the mortuary.

Later, driving home from the mortuary, Lucas says, "You won't believe what I found in a cardboard box in Scorch's room. It's too creepy to tell you."

Gracie says, "Tell me, or I'll stop the car."

Lucas holds his hand over his mouth, Gracie stops the car in the middle of the street. "Gracie, just drive and I'll tell you, but you're going to want off this case when you hear."

"Go on, Lucas, tell me." Gracie begs.

"Packed inside a cardboard box, Scorch had a bunch of glass jars. I picked up one of them, and it was filled with human teeth! I don't want to imagine what other human parts were in the other jars."

Gracie slams on the brakes, nearly sending Lucas through the windshield. Gracie starts to gag.

Lucas looks over at her and says, "Oh no, here we go again."

13

You're Grounded

It's the third day since Tucker's disappearance, and everyone in the town is on high alert. It's all everyone talks about or reads about. It's big news in Fairfax. Parents are starting to keep their kids out of school. Robert Reilly is sitting at the kitchen table reading the local paper. He looks concerned and mumbles to himself, "Fairfax is supposed to be one of the safest neighborhoods in Marin County. How could this happen here?" Gracie and Alex walk into the kitchen and sit down at the table. Robert puts the paper down.

Robert says, "Well, hello, you two. Welcome to the land of the living."

Gracie says, "Hi, Mr. Reilly."

"Hi, Dad," Alex says. "What's new in the paper? Did they find Tucker yet?"

Gracie looks up, obviously very interested in Robert's answer.

"No, but they have a suspect."

Gracie and Alex both stand up and rush over to where Robert is sitting, practically knocking him over to get to the paper. Robert feels ambushed by them.

"Whoa, girls, wait a minute." He grabs the paper and straightens his chair.

"Go on, Dad, read it to us. Don't miss a word. Please."

"*Tobias Wallace, age 60, of Fairfax, California, was arrested by two Central police officers late last night for suspected arson. Mr. Wallace is no newcomer to arson. He is now under investigation for arson and kidnapping after a full search of his room by forensics came up with gasoline cans, incendiary materials, and other damaging evidence, including a blood-stained jacket that could link Mr. Wallace to Tucker Baron's disappearance.*"

Alex interrupts. "Dad, is there a picture of Toby?"

"Yes."

"Show us, please."

He turns the paper around to show them. They both gasp.

Alex says, "He's so scary and so guilty looking. I'm betting he's got Tucker tied up in his basement."

Robert says, "Hold it right there, Alex. You don't know anything about him."

Frustrated, Alex says, "But I do, Dad. He works with Lucas."

Robert drops the paper on the table and spills his coffee. He walks over to the stairs and yells, "Lucas, come down here this instant."

Patricia comes running in. "What did you say, Alex?"

"I said Lucas works with that guy. He runs the oven at the crematorium."

"What!" Both parents cry. "Lucas, come down here now!"

Lucas comes racing into the kitchen. He stops short as he sees Gracie standing there in her pajamas. He feels embarrassed, like his parents know that they almost kissed and how much he likes her.

"What's up?" he says, trying to act cool. Patricia motions for Alex and Gracie to go upstairs. Gracie smiles nervously at Lucas as she passes him.

His parents take him into the living room to the sofa, but Lucas refuses to sit down. And he refuses to quit his job.

"I need the money. I want to save up to buy a car."

Robert says, "I understand, but you absolutely can not work at the crematorium anymore."

Lucas answers defiantly, "Well, I am."

"Then you're grounded." Robert's cell phone rings. He says to Patricia, "I've got to get this, but I'll be right back. He leaves the room.

Patricia is visibly upset. She's never seen Lucas this way. "Lucas, where is your head? Do you need to see Dr. Harris, your sister's therapist? Seriously, what's going on upstairs there." Lucas looks blankly at his mom as she taps his head. "I mean, something is terribly wrong with someone your age wanting to work with dead people. Are you depressed?"

Lucas doesn't hear her. He's thinking about how he can't quit the mortuary. He'd lose his reason to be with Gracie, plus he really does want to find the kidnapper and save Tucker. He's got to get out of the house tonight somehow.

"Mom, I have homework."

"Lucas, that excuse is lame. You know your father's grounded you. Go up to your room now."

Lucas, who is still continuing to figure out a plan for his escape tonight, says, "Sure, Mom, whatever." Then he takes two stairs at a time as he rushes to get upstairs.

He hurries to Alex's room and knocks. Gracie opens the door. The smile on her face lets Lucas know she's glad to see him.

Lucas says, "Could I talk to you for a minute." Gracie follows him into his room.

Before Lucas has a chance to speak, Gracie blurts out, "Lucas, now that Toby Wallace is behind bars, and with all that damaging evidence against him, especially Tucker's blood-stained jacket, all they need is a confession from him, which I'm sure is imminent. The case is pretty well sewn up. I'm almost finished with my criminology paper, so I'll be heading back to school tomorrow." Gracie adds sadly, "The thing is, Lucas, I didn't count on feeling so bad for Tucker and his family. I even feel bad for the old guy, Toby. I actually feel an emotional attachment to all the people involved in Tucker's disappearance."

She looks directly at Lucas, who doesn't look away. They both think yeah, especially you. Gracie has tears in her eyes.

Lucas walks over to Gracie and gives her a hug. "I feel bad, too, but Gracie, the case isn't closed. That's what I wanted to talk to you about. Scorch is not guilty. They have the wrong man. The kidnapper is still out there. I know it. I can feel it in my bones. Scorch may be rude, he is old, and obsessed with fire and the crematorium, but he's not a killer. But someone who works at Morrison's mortuary or a Morrison family member is guilty of a crime. It's a family business. The night I got hit on the head, Scorch wasn't even there, but the oven was turned on."

Lucas is still hugging Gracie. They stay holding each other for a few minutes. Then a bit embarrassed, Lucas finally pulls away. "Gracie, Tucker may still be alive, and we could still find him. I've been thinking about the whole case, and I have another idea."

Gracie dries her eyes and picks up Lucas's Lego Millennium Falcon.

"OK, Han Solo, what's your idea?"

Lucas laughs. "Are you making fun of my Lego spaceship? Or me?" Lucas takes the ship from her. When he tries to put it back on the shelf, he misses it. The ship falls to the floor and breaks apart. Lego bricks go flying across the floor. It's a total nightmare for Lucas in front of Gracie.

Gracie bends down to pick up the Legos off the floor.

Lucas joins her on the floor and says, "Leave it. I was going to take it apart anyway. I'll pick it up later."

Gracie adds, "Lucas, we can rebuild it. I love Legos. All nerds love Legos."

Lucas laughs. "Really, Gracie? You don't have to humor me."

"I'm not, Lucas, you're just smarter and kinder than most boys your age."

Lucas says self-consciously as he holds up one of the bigger spaceship pieces, "Right, I'm just mature for my age."

Gracie sheepishly adds, "And way cuter."

Lucas and Gracie are both sitting on the floor and Lucas leans in and kisses Gracie on the lips very lightly. They both close their eyes. When they break away, Lucas says smiling, with his dimple in full glory, "Let's get back to dealing with Tucker. Here's what I've been thinking."

Gracie listens attentively with a big smile on her face.

"Who swore to Cole when he found out about Vicki and Tucker that he'd get back at Tucker and make his life a nightmare? Who could actually get a hold of the money to pay a hitman to carry that out? Who has a crazy anger control problem? Who has a father who would cover up whatever his son does? Who has the most powerful family in Fairfax? And finally, who did you actually say was our first suspect with a motive?"

Gracie answers immediately. "Brent, Brent, Brent, Brent, Brent, and Brent."

Gracie, grinning at Lucas while patting herself on the back, says, "And who has morphed into the newest Marvel crime fighter? It's Owlman. You know, like Antman."

Lucas laughs. "Gracie, seriously, I think I can prove now that Brent and his accomplice kidnapped Tucker, and he's still alive somewhere. And I think I know just where that is!"

"Oh no you don't. No way! I'm not going back to that haunted mortuary." Gracie stands up and walks over to Lucas's bedroom door and starts to turn the knob to walk out.

Lucas gets on his knees. "Please, Gracie, you don't have to come into the mansion. You can lock the doors and stay in the car. Gracie, if Tucker is still alive, we're his only hope."

"Lucas, that's more direct dialogue from a slasher film and a different girl gets killed when the killer uses his ax to break the locked car door down and he splatters her brains all over the car!" Gracie looks at Lucas's puppy dog face. "OK, fine. But we're bringing your sister, Alex."

Lucas jumps up, smiling. "I have a plan." He takes Gracie's hand and walks her over to his laptop. On the screen is a spreadsheet with a timeline and all the information they have gathered about Tucker's disappearance.

"Wow, this is amazing, Lucas. You really are a born

detective." She keeps reading.

"So are you, Gracie. As you said, we're a great team."

As Gracie gets up, she notices that Webster, the barfinator, looks very lifeless on the floor. He has not left Lucas's side since the attempted murder, and when anyone else is in Lucas's room, Webster is always at full attention.

Gracie bends down to check on Webster, and she gasps when she touches him. "Lucas, Webster is dead. He's not breathing." She starts crying.

Lucas bends down and touches Webster's paralyzed body. He feels for Webster's pulse and sees a handwritten note on his collar. He rips it off and reads it out loud. "Rest in peace, you very bad beast! Lucas, you're next."

Choking back tears, Lucas picks up Webster and heads for the door.

Gracie says loudly after him, "Lucas, you can't tell your parents about Webster or we will be hauled into the police station for questioning." They are both shaken, and Gracie starts crying again. Lucas has turned pale white.

Suddenly, in Lucas's arms, Webster opens his eyes. His tail starts wagging, and he leaps onto Lucas's bed. Gracie and Lucas run over to the bed and hug him. He seems alright. They look at each other and Lucas says, "The kidnapper got close enough to Webster to kill him if he wanted to, he could kill us. He may still be in this house… I was right, Gracie. We are in way over our heads."

14

The Two-Way Mirror

Officer Morrow and Officer Davis are sitting at a table in the interrogation room across from Scorch, who looks particularly banged up and exhausted. His glasses are held together with yellow caution tape, and his face has huge raised red scars that still look raw and painful.

"I didn't start any fire at Morrison's. I swear to you I'm innocent. I don't know any kid named Tucker. I'm not hiding anything. I don't know how that kid's jacket got into my room."

Morrow picks up two glass jars. "What are these, Toby?" Toby's scars seem to get even redder. "I don't know. I never saw them before."

Morrow sits back and says, "Toby, these are human teeth, and we found them in your room. So if you want us to believe you're innocent and had nothing to do with Tucker's kidnapping, then you better tell us the truth."

Toby takes off his glasses and sits quietly for a few seconds. "I collect them from the ashes in the oven and sell them. There's a guy who picks them up from me and pays me for them. It's legal. He pays me extra for the teeth that have gold or silver fillings.

Morrow looks at Davis. "Toby, I'll look into the legal part. I'm not sure how the families of the dead folks who had those teeth would feel about that."

There's a knock on the door. Morrow stands up and gets the door. An officer hands Morrow a note. Morrow leaves the room. She comes back in a few minutes and motions for Davis to come with her.

Officer Davis feels bad for Scorch. "How about some coffee, Toby? What do you want in it?"

"How about a donut?"

Once outside the room, Officer Morrow hands Officer Davis the note. It's the forensic report on the denim jacket they found in Scorch's room. No traces of Scorch's DNA are on the jacket. It's clean. But they found traces of DNA from a Ronald Morrison, a cousin to the Morrison brothers, who's been in and out of the holding cell since he was a teenager and was finally booked about ten years ago for kidnapping his girlfriend. He only served one month and was released.

"I know that character," says Morrow. "He's a loose cannon and dangerous, even though he's never done real time. We have his DNA from a prior, and it matches what forensics took off the kid's bloodied jacket. They both look through the two-way mirror at Scorch.

Davis says, "Poor guy. He may be weird, and he has some history of possible arson a few years back. His whole family was wiped out. There was plenty of damning evidence but no conviction. I personally think he's no arsonist or kidnapper. I think he's been framed to look like he's an arsonist and Tucker's kidnapper. Obviously, whoever framed him knows where that kid Tucker is buried or being hidden."

Officer Morrow adds, "We've got to discharge Toby now. He's not our guy. After the police briefing, let's head back to the mortuary. Maybe we can find more evidence on the funeral director's kid, Brent. I have a strong feeling that the kid is mixed up in Tucker's disappearance, and his phony father is hiding something for him. I just hope it's not a body."

Captain Ward has called for an emergency police briefing at the station. He stands in front of a giant bulletin board with photos, timelines, cross hatches of lines drawn from one picture to another, and in the middle is Tucker Baron's school picture circled in red. All the police officers stand at attention.

"Officers, everything I brief you on today is fully detailed in the report on your desks." He walks up to the billboard. "This is our timeline, and what we know so far about what happened to Tucker since he went missing on October 26."

All the officers look at the written report.

"I know we're all frustrated with this investigation," Captain Wade continues, "but as you can read, most of our leads and information on Tucker's whereabouts has basically led us nowhere. The alleged kidnapper, possible killer, is still out there on the loose. Please follow up every bit of information. No lead is too small not to follow up. Our kids here in Fairfax are in real danger from this maniac."

He points to Toby Wallace's picture, which is pinned up next to Brent Morrison's school picture. "We brought in our number-one suspect, Toby Wallace, for questioning and after a lengthy and thorough interrogation by Officers Morrow and Officer Davis, we concluded that he is no longer a chief suspect and should be released. We will keep him under surveillance for possible arson, but at this time there's not enough critical evidence to link him to Tucker Baron's disappearance. He's not our guy."

One officer raises his hand. "Yes, Officer Meeker."

Meeker says, "I don't get it. This Wallace guy is a psycho and known arsonist. Officer Morrow found the missing kid's jacket in Wallace's room. That's strong evidence to me. Why would you release him when we have no other suspect?"

"Officer Meeker, did you not read the report that you're holding in front of your face? Do you need glasses or maybe a Seeing-Eye dog?" Anyone else have a problem? Or are you all looking for a desk job? Read my lips, there was no DNA from Toby Wallace on the kid's jacket. Zilch! Nada!"

Annoyed, Captain Ward continues, "Please hold all questions until the end of my briefing." Captain Ward holds up Tucker's jacket in a plastic bag as he walks over to the crime board and pins up the mugshot of Ronald Morrison. "Officers, most of you will recognize this lowlife, Ronald Morrison, who is a long-standing criminal and convicted felon for kidnapping his girlfriend back in 2005. His DNA and fingerprints were still dancing all over the missing kid's jacket when forensics gave us their report."

The captain rubs his chin in frustration. "Unfortunately, Ronald Morrison is part of the Morrison family, so he's well connected and a potential flight risk. We need more evidence to bring him in and keep him behind bars. All the Morrisons are made of Teflon and convictions mysteriously don't stick." He circles Ronald's picture in bold red.

"We don't think Morrison acted alone. He has no motive. We think he was hired by someone as a hitman. So who has a motive? Who wanted this kid, Tucker Baron,"—using his wooden pointer to tap on Tucker's picture—"out of the way? And who hired Ronald to do just that? That's what we need to find out ASAP if we want to find the Baron kid alive. Officers Morrow and Officer Davis, you stake out the Morrisons Chapel and Crematorium. Officers Lawrence and Cleeker, you cover Fairfax

High School. Officers Drew and Samson, please check out the USC campus. There was a break-in in the science lab and there were ashes all over the floor. Maybe human ashes, who knows. There may be some connection to this case. Officers Howard and Kellog, you stake out Matt Morrison's house. I'm thinking he may be the guy that hired his cousin Ronald to do the dirty work. I just don't know why he would want this kid kidnapped. The rest of you, please stay vigilant. This kid's life is in our hands. Make sure I get full reports by the end of the day or call in any leads. That's all for now. Dismissed."

They all say in unison,"Yes, sir!"

While the emergency meeting is going on at the police station, Matt Morrison drives up to the Morrison mansion alone and goes inside. He locks the front door and rushes to the back. Through another secret door, he climbs up a set of backstairs. At the top, then down a hall, he opens a door. It's dark, but there's a little dim light.

Surprise, surprise. There. with a bandage on his head and out cold, is Tucker Baron, the missing teen. Sitting across from the bed, smoking a cigarette, is the guy that kidnapped him, who's name is RIP, as in Rest in Peace. Matt is aware that Rip, who's real name is Ronald, is definitely a psycho, but he's been a fixer for the Morrison family for years, and he's Matt's cousin. He's a Morrison. Always a bully and a screw up, Ronald

Morrison should be under psychiatric care. Lately, Matt has become increasingly fearful of Ronald.

Ronald is sitting on a chair polishing his black, pointy shoes with love and fury.

"Ronald, what's with those shoes?" Matt asks.
"They were my dad's, you know, Charlie Morrison, the guy who knew too much about the Morrison clan. The one that was murdered in cold blood right here in this building. You remember him, Cuz, don't you?"

Matt, not wanting to get Ronald riled, says, "Sure, I remember Cousin Charlie. He's the guy who ran off with the Morrison family reunion dues."

Ronald keeps polishing furiously, "You know, Cuz, it's just a matter of time before the police find us. I say we fire that Tucker kid up now."

"Ronald, you say that about every one."

Angrily, Ronald says, "Don't ever call me Ronald." As he's now furiously polishing his knife. "Rip is my name, and will be yours, too, if you call me anything else."

At the Reilly's house, Gracie walks into Alex's bedroom. "Alex, get your coat, it's 'go' time, or whatever they say on crime shows. Scorch could be Brent's accomplice. I want to find evidence that proves otherwise. I know this guy is a weirdo, but he's not a killer. Scorch is in jail right now, so it's perfect timing to check out his house. Alex, seriously, I feel like we're real spies."

Alex grabs her coat and formerly ashy car keys, having practically soaked them in bleach, still holding them out like something that died. "Yeah, like the Black Widow."

"Wait, which one of us is the Black Widow?"

Gracie says, "I am."

"No, I am." She holds up the formerly ashy keys. Alex, still grimacing from touching the keys, says, "What about Lucas? Won't he want to come with us?"

Gracie says, "No, this is something I want to bring to the table myself."

They run down the back stairs and out the door. "Gracie, how do you know where Toby lives?"

"I have my ways. I'm not just a pretty face. They both laugh. Gracie is definitely feeling more confident. They arrive at the house about ten minutes later. The house is totally dark and vacant.

Gracie takes out a credit card to slide in the door frame, which she's seen done a hundred times in movies, but when she touches the door, it swings open. They both turn on their flashlights on their phones.

The house is small and looks like no one has lived there in years. Alex walks around, shining her flashlight on different objects. She shines her flashlight on the fireplace and sees a framed family photo on the mantel. She looks closer. There's a picture of a young man with his arm around a young woman, and she has her arms around two young girls.

"Gracie, come here." They look at the photo together. "It's Scorch when he was younger, and he's smiling. This must be his family."

Gracie continues walking around and stumbles across a desk. She opens the top drawer. There are tons of old bills and a worn newspaper clipping.

The Fairfax Times

November 24, 1994

A tragic fire swept through the home of Tobias Wallace, a Fairfax fireman, the night before Thanksgiving, and took the life of his wife and two daughters. Mr. Wallace was fighting another fire at the time, but still managed to run into his house fully engulfed in flames, against orders, to try and rescue his wife and two daughters, ages 4 and 7. He was severely burned on his face and hands.

After a police investigation, the fire was determined to be suspicious. But the police could not find enough evidence of arson. Toby Wallace was held on suspicion of arson after incendiary materials were found in his home. He was never arrested and denied any wrongdoing.

"I loved my family. This is the biggest tragedy in my life. I

will never recover. I am innocent." The fire is under investigation with Toby Wallace remaining a prime suspect.

Please send all donations and flowers to the Morrison Chapel and Crematorium by the Bay on Sharon Street.

Just as Gracie finishes reading the article out loud, they hear someone at the front door. Gracie folds up the article and puts it in her coat. Gracie pulls Alex into the kitchen.

A man's voice booms. "Who's there? Why don't you leave me alone. I didn't do anything. I'm innocent. I've always been innocent!"

They hear footsteps approaching the kitchen. Gracie grabs Alex and instinctively walks down a few steps and opens the door to the garage. They both look around before they escape through the garage door and see lots of pyro equipment and gasoline cans, which look a lot like an arsonists' home or someone who's planning to blow themselves up.

Flashback:
Wednesday at 10:00 p.m. the night Tucker disappeared

Tucker has his hands tied behind his back. His mouth is taped shut. He's in the mortuary's icebox, where dead bodies are kept until they're buried or cremated. He's shaking uncontrollably. It's dark, and there are cadavers in there with him. In between shivering, he's whimpering.

He hears a noise that he thinks is coming from one of the cadavers. He stands up ready to run or fight, he's seen a lot of zombie films, so he knows what comes next: the zombies will come at him through doors, windows, other rooms. He thinks he hears voices outside. The door handle turns. The door opens a bit, and he thinks he sees a shadow of a zombie on the wall. He jumps and then falls backward. He goes down hard with a loud THUD when he hits his head on the cement floor.

The door opens wider. Brent struts into the room. "Thought you needed some cooling off, asshole." Brent sees Tucker's lifeless body on the floor and rushes over to it. "Crap, I killed him! I scared him to death!"

15

Breaking News

Matt Morrison is watching TV with his wife, Karen. The news street reporter is interviewing people on Main Street in Fairfax.

TV reporter: "How do you feel now that the alleged kidnapper, Toby Wallace, is behind bars?"

Woman on the street: "So much safer. I can let my kids go out and play again. I can relax."

TV reporter: "Sir, how do you feel now about Toby Wallace's capture right here in your neighborhood?"

Man on the street: "I heard that the missing kid's jacket was in the kidnapper's bedroom. And it had blood all over it."

TV reporter: "Miss, what do you think about the capture of the alleged child kidnapper right in your own backyard?"

Young woman: "Wait, the guy that kidnapped that kid buried him in my backyard? How Could that be? I work at home."

TV reporter: "I didn't say that, miss. Not in your backyard.

That's not what I said...wait fake news!"

Suddenly at the bottom of the TV screen...

BREAKING NEWS...Mr. Toby Wallace, age 60, has been released for lack of evidence in the kidnapping of Tucker Baron, who is still missing. If anyone has any information on Tucker Baron's whereabouts, please call 911 or contact the Central police station at 415-555-7777.

Matt jumps up off his couch and screams at the TV set. "Crap! Crap! Crap! Scorch was the perfect fall guy. Now what am I going to do?" He screams up the stairs. "Brent! Get down here this minute!"

Brent comes running down the stairs and into the living room. Matt's red in the face and trying to contain his violent temper, so instead he puts on a fake smile that is scarier to Brent then when his dad is actually screaming at him.

"Brent, you started this whole mess by hiring your psychotic cousin Ronald to scare that kid, Tucker. So you're going to help me get that kid back home and apologize to him and his family and hope they don't press charges. Get your coat."

Brent is scared stiff of his dad and follows his dad's orders.

Matt kisses Karen on her cheek. "Don't wait for me for dinner, but keep that chicken fired up." He smiles and winks. "We may be very late tonight."

Brent mumbles to himself. "Disgusting."

Ronald, in the upstairs bedroom at the Morrison mansion, is watching the same news report that Matt was watching at home. Tucker is still sleeping in a bed across from Ronald. The doctor, Victor Morrison, cousin Vic, who comes twice a day to check on Tucker, has just left. He says the kid had a concussion, but he sedated him. He'll be OK to go home tomorrow, as long as he doesn't hit his head."

Ronald has been ruminating for days about the situation. He knows he'll be the only one held responsible for kidnapping that kid. He'll go to jail for a long time once the kid is released and brought home. His cousins, the twins Matt and Jerry, were always as bad as he was, they just never got caught. He also knows that his cousin judge Clark Morrison, aka Superman to him, will never help him out. Ronald used to whack him around as kids.

So he's one hundred percent on his own. If he's found guilty, he'll be sent away for a long time unless he gets rid of the evidence. He walks over to Tucker's bed and looks at the kid sleeping. "I'm going to take you down to the oven and fire you up. So there will be no body. And no body means no jail! It's that simple. I'm going to take care of this myself this time."

Ronald is pumped and mad…crazy mad. He leaves the room at lightning speed and heads to the basement. He makes his way stealthily through the corridors until he reaches the crematory room. He takes out a keyring with tons of keys and opens the doors leading to the crematory chamber oven. The crematory room is lit only by the red glow of the "EMERGENCY" signs above the exit doors. Right in front of him is the oven chamber with two giant steel doors. The chamber itself is menacing.

Without time to waste, Ronald finds the operating controls next to the chamber. There's a sign above the controls with detailed instructions and the word "WARNING" written in big red letters. Ronald rushes through reading the instructions, finds the "ON" switch and pulls it down. The oven roars ON and the rumble of its power shakes the room. Ronald is thrown back to the wall from the amount of energy that is released. The sound of the powerful engine is so noisy that Ronald covers his ears. He realizes he may have to lower the thermostat, but when he tries to, the digital temperature control only moves up higher, from 1200 degrees to 1400 degrees. He holds his ears and heads for the door. When he looks back at the digital thermostat, it reads "1600 degrees." On his way out, he thinks. *So, cousin Matt, how would you like Tucker cooked? Rare or well done? I think it will have to be well done this time.*

16

Your Son Is Missing

A sliver of the moon gives just enough light to make out the Morrison Mansion as Matt drives up to the front. He looks up at the big engraved archway sign—THE MORRISONS CHAPEL AND CREMATORIUM BY THE BAY—and says to Brent, "Get out of the car."

Brent gets out of the car slowly and stands next to his father, not knowing what to expect. "Brent, you're my only son. All this will be yours someday, I need you to promise me one thing."

Brent nervously says, "Of course, Dad."

"You will bulldoze this friggin place to the ground!"

Upstairs, inside the mansion, Ronald is just finishing wrapping up Tucker's body in a white sheet like a mummy. Hearing a car drive up, he panics, knowing he has to get Tucker down to the crematorium before Matt comes up to Tucker's room. Underestimating the weight of the wrapped body and overestimating his own strength, when Ronald picks up the body, it immediately slips through his hands and makes a big -THUD when Tucker lands on his head. Breathing heavily, Ronald lifts the body off the floor, but the body is too top heavy, so Ronald and the body go over backward making another big -THUD when Tucker hits his head on the floor—again!

"Crap, I'm going to kill Matt after I fry this kid." He lets out a loud huff from down in his belly from sheer anger and frustration, which actually powers him up to grab the body, put it on his shoulder like a sack of flour, and walk out the door. You can hear him huffing as he walks down the stairs.

A police car with its lights off parks down the street from Morrison's Funeral home. Officers Morrow and Davis get out of the car. They walk up the street and duck into the Morrison's yard. The officers are trying not to alert anyone to their presence to avoid suspects from fleeing the mansion.

They find a back door and kick it open.

At the same time, Scorch is sleeping in his back room of the building. The gasoline cans are still on his floor. A loud -THUD from upstairs wakes him. He grabs an urn as a weapon from a shelf near his bed. "I swear, one of you jerky kids is going to end up in this urn when I catch you." He heads out the door and down the hall holding the urn.

Going out the front door right then, Alex yells to her mom, "Mom, Gracie needs a few things at the drugstore to take back to school, like Q-tips, Band-Aids, lipstick, Kleenex, and tampons."

Her mother yells back, "Alex, too much information. See you later. Drive safely."

As Alex goes out the front door, Lucas sneaks down the back stairs. He's left his music on in his room. When he gets to the bottom of the stairs, Webster is waiting for him. He starts barking. "Please, Webster, have a heart." Webster keeps barking. Lucas feels in his pants pocket and finds some old skittles. He throws them into the other room and Webster takes off. Lucas quickly runs out the back door and jumps into the back seat of the waiting car in the driveway.

Alex screams, then yells at him, "You scared the bejesus out of me, you doofus."

Gracie just laughs and looks at Lucas. Alex notices a definite buzz between them. She says to herself, "I knew it."

As they pull away, a car's headlights come to life. The Central police logo on the door of the car can be seen as it follows Lucas and the girls.

Patricia walks up the stairs with a tray of food to bring to Lucas. She feels bad that maybe they were too hard on him, but she grimaces at the thought of him working with a possible kidnapper.

"We may owe Lucas an apology," she says to herself. "He really didn't do anything wrong." She knocks on his door. No answer. The music is very loud. She knocks again. No answer. "Lucas, it's Mom. I'm coming in."

She walks in. The music is blaring. The room is empty. She does a quick look around the room and sees that Lucas's laptop is open. She looks at the screen. Her eyes open wider and wider as she keeps reading. "What?! My son has been secretly investigating Tucker's disappearance and was attacked by a man with a knife." She gasps. "And Gracie was followed by the possible kidnapper. Alex and Gracie broke into Toby Wallace's house? She is so grounded. College or no college. Putting both of their lives in danger." Patricia is in shock "Lucas, what have you done?" She goes to the top of the stairs and yells downstairs.

"Robert, come up here this instant! Your son is missing!" She pulls out her phone and makes a call. "Noreen, get Barbara and Sandy right now. Lucas has disappeared, and he's in danger." Patricia looks back at the laptop screen. "But luckily, I know where to find him." She's looking at the last words he wrote. "The Morrison Chapel and Crematorium by the Bay."

17

The Ghost Of Funerals Past

Matt and Brent are the first to enter the Morrison mansion. Matt leads Brent upstairs. Matt opens the door to the room that Tucker was being held in, but the room is empty. There's a cigarette still burning in an ashtray.

Matt shifts into high gear and races around the room, checking the closet, under the bed, and accidentally knocks the burning cigarette out of the ashtray and into a waste paper basket that's holding one of Ronald's shoe polishing rags. The rags start to smoke immediately.

There is no Tucker or Ronald in the room. Red faced, Matt grabs Brent by his jacket. "This is all your fault!"

"I'm sorry, Dad. I have a bad temper and—

CRASH!

Matt, still holding onto Brent's jacket, pulls him to the stairs and races down them. On the stairs, Matt catches himself from falling as he trips over a set of keys on one of the stairs. He picks them up and shows them to Brent. "These are

Ronald's keys to the crematorium, and Ronald was dead set on killing Tucker to hide the evidence. I'll bet he's taken the kid to the crematorium. You better pray that Ronald is too dumb to work the new oven, or we're all cooked."

Brent appears white as a ghost.

Second to enter Morrison's, Officers Morrow and Davis have split up as they separately check out the different rooms in the mortuary. Suddenly a flash of white, like a ghost, floats by in the dark. Officer Davis jumps back and bumps into a table with a vase, which crashes to the floor. Davis has also heard about the Morrison mansion murder and the haunting of the victim. He pulls out his gun and yells, "Morrow, I swear on my mother, I just saw a ghost!"

Morrow comes into the room. "Davis, it's just your nerves." She clocks something white ahead of her. She takes off down the hall. He follows. She yells, "Put your gun away, Davis, or you'll end up shooting me."

Scorch hears the crash and keeps walking toward the crematorium. He's still carrying an urn. He also sees the white sheet running by.

He shouts, "Finally, I've been waiting for years to see one of those."

Lucas enters the building through the back entrance with

his key. He had instructed Alex and Gracie to wait in the car until he signaled them to come inside. He's standing in the hall leading to the crematorium, when something white rushes by and yells, "Help!"

Lucas steps in to get a closer look and sees that the white bundle is being carried by a big guy wearing shiny, black, pointy dress shoes.

Hey, those shoes belong to the guy who tried to kill me, Lucas thinks. He shouts, "Stop!" as he takes after him.

Ronald stops at the crematorium. He tries the doors. They're locked. He reaches into his pocket for his keys. No keys! He searches in his other pocket. Still no keys! He must have left them upstairs. In a panic, he uses the top of the white covered bundle—Tucker's head—as a ramming rod. After many tries, the locked doors open, and he heads inside. Lucas, close behind, follows him in. Ronald grabs a gurney by the door and throws the white covered body on it as the crematorium doors shut again automatically.

Scorch arrives at the crematorium doors right after Lucas. He hears the power of the crematory chamber oven on at full blast. Shaking his head in despair, he tries the doors. They're locked. He goes for his keys in his pocket when Officer Morrow yells, "Hold it right there, buddy."

Scorch keeps attempting to repeat, "I have to fix the thermostat lever on the oven," but his stammering from the dangerous situation is making his words all jumbled.

He rambles on. "They just installed a new electric crematory chamber oven three days ago, and it's crap. They were in such a hurry to get the new, cheaper oven up and working that they didn't empty out the gas line from the old gas chamber. If the excess gas from the gas pipe line touches the burning ashes, we will all go *POOF*"—he makes a hand gesture—"all of us!"

"Just calm down and step away from the doors, Toby," Officer Morrow demands.

"It must be two thousand degrees inside the chamber right now. The thermostat gets stuck when the oven goes over 1600 degrees, which is the normal temperature inside the chamber. It's a fire safety precaution, but it doesn't work right. I begged them, I pleaded, I told them, the new oven is dangerous unless you are trained to work on them. The last person that turned the new oven on is responsible for putting all our lives in jeopardy. That's who you police should be after, not me."

Officer Davis, sweating profusely, says, "OK, oven master, please turn around first, so we can straighten this all out."

Scorch gets more upset. "I have the keys. Listen to me, I have to shut the oven down."

Officer Davis moves toward Scorch, who panics and throws the urn that he's carrying at him, knocking Officer Davis down.

Officer Morrow yells at Scorch. "Stand right there, Toby. You're under arrest for hitting a police officer and resisting arrest." She bends down to check if Davis is breathing, still pointing her gun at Scorch. She stands up and says, "Luckily for you, Toby, my partner is OK."

At that moment, Scorch turns toward the steel doors, and before Officer Morrow can do anything, he uses his keys to unlock the doors, then goes in. Officer Morrow closely follows him inside.

18

The Crematorium

It is dangerously hot inside the crematorium room, which is filled with a smoky red haze from the big red EMERGENCY sign above the doors. The chamber oven emits puffs of smoke as it continues to rumble loudly like a hungry monster. Scorch runs over to the oven thermostat. The temperature of the chamber is as he expected: two thousand degrees. He tries to move the thermostat control lever, but it won't budge. *"I told them this new electric oven can malfunction easily,"* Scorch rants to himself, *"No one ever listens to me."*

Officer Morrow, who's standing near Storch, hears a man's gravelly voice and moves in closer. It's smoky, but she can make out who the man is. It's Ronald Morrison. He looks just like his mug shot, and he's holding a knife at a tall kid's throat. She also notices a bulky white sheet on a gurney next to him. She draws her gun and yells, "Drop the knife or I'll shoot."

Ronald shouts, "Go ahead, lady, fire your gun. But this kid will die first."

Suddenly out of nowhere, another voice says, "Ronald, drop the knife. This won't end well for any of us if you don't. We're family, and I promise you I'll do whatever I can to help you get out of this mess, but not if you hurt that boy." It's Matt Morrison speaking. He's standing behind Officer Morrow with Brent, who is scared stiff.

"Nice try, Cuz, but you never helped before. You could have helped me all these years, but you didn't. So I'm going to go out in style and bring this kid with me."

The five of them stand frozen, afraid to make a move and set off Ronald. Officer Morrow, standing the closest, sees through the red smoky haze that Ronald has started to draw blood at Lucas's neck. The look in Lucas's eyes is pure terror, knowing he can't wiggle out of this one. Lucas closes his eyes, expecting the worst, when Ronald, with his knife still at Lucas's neck, pitches forward onto the cement floor. He barely misses cutting Lucas's carotid artery as Lucas also falls forward. Tucker, still half-covered in a white sheet, steps forward holding a crematorial urn he just used on Ronald's head. Still high from medication, he grins. "Wow, this has been the best horror film I've ever seen!"

Without warning, a loud hissing inside the crematory chamber escapes and the chamber door pops open. Burning ashes start spurting out like lava from an erupting volcano. Scorch, eyes glued to the oven, yells, "Everyone out before it blows!"

Officer Morrow reacts quickly and hustles everyone towards the emergency doors. Officer Davis, who has quickly recovered, is standing with her. He picks up Ronald from the floor and taps Matt to help him carry the unconscious Ronald toward the doors.

Scorch, still at the thermostat, says to himself, *"I'm not leaving until this is fixed. I must find the gas line."* As Lucas and Brent are being ushered out, Brent is actually helping Lucas walk. They hear Scorch's mutterings and see him struggling with the thermostat. They both walk over to him. Seeing both of the boys coming toward him out of the red haze, and delirious from the heat, he's convinced they are superheroes, who have come to save the day. "Over here, Superman. You fix the lever while I head to the back wall to find the gas line." Lucas and Brent, although already in bad shape, stay back to help Scorch.

When Scorch turns to leave them, he looks down and sees with horror that the red-hot embers from the chamber are making a snake-like path directly to the area where the old gas line is located. Hurriedly, Scorch feels his way along a back wall behind the new oven. He wheezes as he makes his way. Scorch's breathing is labored. He watches the embers burning like lava. He feels his legs getting heavier, like he has to lie down. No oxygen. *I'm a fireman. I can do this.* He's about to faint when he sees the gas line pipe, but he has to sit down...

19

Secret Doors

Outside the mansion, a curious crowd of onlookers have started gathering. Fire trucks with sirens screaming, race into the parking lot with firemen jumping off the trucks before the engines stop. A mass of police cars arrive at breakneck speed, and the bomb squad heads directly inside. The mansion area is lit up like a movie premiere. Sirens are wailing and red lights are whirling as a hose is directed at the fire in an upstairs bedroom.

Standing in front of Alex's car, Gracie and Alex are watching in horror as they see the bomb squad arrive. The police are rushing to put up barricades in front of the mansion to cut off any access.

"I'm going in there now to get Lucas," Gracie says to Alex.

"Then I'm going with you. He is my brother, after all."

Gracie adds, "And he is my boy—"

"Your what?" Alex interrupts.

Gracie says, "My boy brother."

Gracie thinks about what to do to get inside. "I've got it,

Alex. Just follow my lead and do what I say."

Alex looks over at Gracie. "Now who's the bad ass?"

They walk over to the barricade. Alex pretends to faint in front of a policeman. While he's helping her, Gracie ducks under the barricade and runs to the back of the building. It's dark and so much is going on that no one notices her. Alex makes a quick recovery, so when the policeman walks away, she makes a run for it. They meet up at the back door and slip inside.

Robert, Patricia and her three sisters drive up and jump out of their car. Patricia hits the pavement yelling, "Let me through, please. My son is in there, and I'm a nurse."

The three sisters also keep yelling, "Please let us through, we're nurses."

Robert runs after them shouting, "Let the nurses through, it's an emergency."

They try to break through the barricade. Two officers they know stop them. One puts his arm around Patricia and tries calming her down. He says gently, "We're doing everything we can, Patty, just be ready for him when he comes out." Robert and the sisters surround Patty, understanding the danger if any of them races into the mansion right now. None of them know that Alex and Gracie are in the mansion too.

At that moment inside, Gracie shines her flashlight on the sign above the Mortuary Storage Room, a chill runs up Gracie's spine when she sees that the door is wide open. She shines the flashlight inside and sees the rows of urns and thinks of Lucas. That makes her smile. The flashlight makes the urns cast big shadows on the wall. Alex gasps at the sight of the urns and turns to the door to run out. Gracie grabs Alex's sweater as she's about to bolt.

"Seriously, Alex, it's just a few urns. Lucas likes talking to them." Alex, rolling her eyes, says, "Well, Lucas is a mental case."

CRASH! One of the three unclaimed urns falls off the shelf and hits the floor. Both girls scream and run out.

Gracie grabs Alex's hand and leads her down a hall to the crematorium. Gracie turns around quickly when she sees the bomb squad team working on the locked crematorium doors. Gracie quickly pulls Alex by her sweater in another direction. Alex is fighting to get away.

The corridor is dark and the power is off, but luckily, the other night when Gracie was here with Lucas, it was also dark. With Gracie's great memory for detail, the hallway looks familiar. They come across one of the secret doors Lucas proudly showed Gracie as he shared some historical stuff about the mansion.

Gracie opens the door hoping to find the crematorium. Instead she finds a room with dozens of fuse boxes, which she recognizes because her dorm at school is ancient and always losing power from all the plugged-in hairdryers. The cries that come from her fellow dorm-mates when the power goes out is so deafening and annoying that she took it upon herself to become the fastest fuse fixer in the dorm. She exits this room in a hurry.

She finds another door that opens upon a room filled to the ceiling with funeral apparatus, gurneys, urns, etc. Gracie closed that door quickly as Alex begins to gag.

Finally, Gracie finds another door that she opens and is immediately enveloped into a big hot cloud of red smoke. Gracie and Alex gasp from the shock and extreme heat and head in. It's obviously the crematorium. Ahead in the red smoke-filled room, they can barely make out who's there. They see a lone figure who seems to be standing at attention and talking to themselves. As they get closer, they also see another body lying on the floor near the standing figure. Gracie's heart beats faster. Alex is in tears as they approach slowly. As they get closer, it's still too smoky to make out whose body is lying on the floor.

Alex says to Gracie, "You go see who it is. I can't move."

Gracie, now in tears, walks over to the motionless body and bends down to the floor to get a closer look. She sees now that it is Brent. She shouts, "It's not Lucas," then checks Brent's pulse. He's alive. When he opens his eyes, she says gently, "Stay still, save your breath, we will get you out of here."

Lucas, delirious from the heat, has been standing in a trancelike state near Brent's body ever since Scorch went to find the gas line. After repeatedly trying to release the lever on the thermostat to lower the oven temperature, Brent has succumbed to heat exhaustion and fainted, which left Lucas standing at the thermostat lever, like a brave captain going down with his sinking ship. With his hands still on the lever, he mumbles to himself, "Now that I'm facing death…" Probably a speech he took from one of his sci-fi books.

Someone yells, "Lucas!" which jars him out of his trance and stops his mumblings. Looking out through the red haze and smoke, with sweat dripping into his eyes, he sees a shape in front of him. As the shape gets closer, he still can't make out who's there but the figure is getting closer and closer… and then the figure yells, "LUCAS" and he recognizes Gracie's voice. He yells, "GRACIE" and runs over and hugs and kisses her on the lips and she kisses him back. He drenches her in his sweat, but she holds on.

Alex runs over now, too, and hugs him but backs off quickly. "Ugh, little bro, you stink." Alex's voice jolts Lucas back to the reality of the danger they're facing.

Before Lucas can say anything, Alex screams as she looks down and sees the glowing embers flowing across the floor. Gracie grabs Lucas. Lucas looks down too.

"We're in big trouble if those ashes ignite the gas in the pipeline," Lucas shouts over the rumbling of the oven. "Scorch said the whole place will blow."

Gracie stares at Lucas, and without saying a word, takes off. She runs out of the crematorium door back into the hall. Lucas yells, "Gracie come back."

Meanwhile, Scorch is getting closer to the gas line. As the master of the oven and a former fireman, he's cleaned out the gas lines for years, but he also sees that the burning ashes are getting closer. He grabs the line. He inspects it, then tries pushing it back into the wall. *I have no time. I have no time.* He uses all of his strength and pushes. *I can't fail again.*

Gracie at the same time finds the door that had all the fuses. She knows what to do and starts furiously pulling the boxes open and flipping the switches up and down. She lets out a groan after she realizes there are too many fuses and too little time. It's dark, and Gracie's having trouble breathing from the fire upstairs in the mansion. *C'mon, Gracie, this is what you wished for. Here's the excitement, the adventure, the bad ass, a whole different me. I can do this. I have to do this.* Without much hope and with lots of sweat, she gets to the last fuse box. On the very first fuse, she pulls down.

As if orchestrated on cue by a grand maestro, Scorch lifts the gas line to where it's safe, and the rumble of the ovens stops. Scorch passes out and falls to the floor.

Outside, the crowd cheers as some of the lights go on and off in the mansion, and strange funeral organ music floats over the crowd.

20

See You At Christmas

The autumn night has turned cold with the moon finally making a full show. The scene outside Morrison's mansion is still chaotic. The crowd is dispersing. The fire engines are roaring out of the area with their sirens still wailing. The red lights from the police cars are whirling and creating a red cast over the whole building. Four ambulances are parked in the lot amid a lot of activity. The back doors are open in the ambulances.

In one of the ambulances, Scorch is lying on a gurney with an oxygen mask over his face and an IV hooked up to his arm. His eyes are closed. The doctor said he should be OK, but they recommended a brief stay in the hospital where he can be observed. Scorch refuses a hospital stay and is driven to his own home with an attending nurse.

Brent is in another ambulance, and he too has an oxygen mask on his face and an IV in his arm, but he's sitting up. Matt and Karen are sitting with him. Karen's phone rings, and she moves away. Everyone looks upset.

In the third ambulance, Tucker is attached to an IV, and he's still grinning from too much medication. Vicki is holding his hand. His parents are filling out forms and look to be in shock but smiling.

Surrounded by Patricia and Robert and Patricia's three sisters, Lucas and Alex both come out of the fourth ambulance. They are covered in shiny plastic space sheets, but they appear to be alright. Gracie follows right behind them wrapped in a space sheet, as well. Alex runs back to get her and bring her into her family's fold. She's smiling. Walking along with them is Officer Morrow. Officer Davis is busy taking statements from all the witnesses that he and Officer Morrow will be writing-up back at the station.

The Central police are controlling the crowd and making sure everyone is dispersing safely. The parking area is illuminated in the dark by the spotlights from a TV crew that has set up. Except for the absence of a ton of dead bodies and blood flowing everywhere, the parking lot looks exactly like the final scene in a gory slasher film.

A reporter with a television crew is trying to get close to the Reilly family as they walk to their cars. Officer Morrow walks over to the reporter and says, "That's enough, buddy, please let this family go home."

The next day, outside on the front lawn at the Reilly's house, it's media madness. Reporters and newscasters are standing and talking to their cameraman. Tucker Baron's kidnapping and rescue by two teens is big news locally and worldwide. One local reporter talks into his microphone. "Two brave teens were able to accomplish what an entire police force could not. How do you like that, America?"

Inside the house, Officers Morrow and Davis have spent the morning taking statements at the dining room table from Lucas, Gracie, and Alex. Webster sits by Lucas wagging his tail. Robert and Patricia and her three sisters sit around the table, as well. Officer Morrow is winding up her assessment of what they should expect from formal criminal charges.

"Despite your heroic acts and helping the police avert further disaster," Officer Morrow says, "you three still technically broke the law by mixing yourselves up in police activity and breaking and entering the Morrison Chapel and Crematorium."

Robert's cell phone rings. He answers it on the first ring and says, "Sorry, I can't talk now, I'm with my family." Lucas smiles as Robert hangs up.

Officer Morrow goes on. "But luckily for you, Matt Morrison and his family are not pressing charges for trespassing, and my superiors are keeping in mind that you helped in the rescue and capture of a wanted criminal for kidnapping and arson. They have agreed to overlook these charges and give you two weeks of community service during your next holiday break." Looking right at Lucas and Gracie. "And you two, from now on, stay out of the detective business. That's our job."

Lucas and Gracie look at each other with a secret smile, knowing this is not the end of their future relationship. Alex looks at them. "Ugh!"

It's two days later. The media circus has mostly disappeared. All three teens slept for hours and ate everything they could when they were awake. Gracie and Alex are in the car ready to go back to school. Lucas hops in the back seat and scares Alex again.

" Lucas, you really are an idiot, but the good kind," Alex says. "Welcome back to the living. All that mortuary dead-guy stuff was scary. I thought I lost my baby brother. You actually developed a heart from all this."

Gracie and Lucas's eyes meet. Gracie notices Lucas isn't wearing his usual flannel shirt. "Nice sweater, Lucas," she says. "OK, you two lovebirds, we gotta go," Alex says.

Gracie says to Lucas, "We did a good job. We saved Tucker, and I wrote a great paper. I'll probably see you on Christmas break."

Lucas says, "Yup."

She goes to kiss him on the cheek but he turns his head

so their lips meet and lock. It's a perfect real kiss. Gracie smiles afterwards.

Lucas jumps out of the car, waves goodbye, and blows a kiss. *Omg, did I just do that? I'm such a freak.*

Alex and Gracie laugh hysterically in the car. Gracie lowers her window and hands Lucas a suitcase. "Don't open it until I leave." She blows him a kiss.

Lucas runs up the stairs and puts the suitcase on his bed, then he looks out the window. Alex's car is gone. Lucas goes to his bed and opens the suitcase. There's a lot of bubble wrap, which is covering three different items. He takes out one of the objects and slowly unravels the bubble wrap. There it is, one of the three unclaimed cremation urns from the mortuary. He looks at the inscription: Marianne Holtz. Grinning, he says, "Welcome home, Marianne."

Epilogue

Six Months Later

The Morrison brothers sold the Morrison Chapel and Crematorium for a loss, and it was quickly turned into a nursing home. Everyone living or working there hears weird noises all the time, and they're all convinced the place is haunted.

Lucas, now 15, found a part-time job in a doctor's office so he can save money for a car. He volunteers at an animal shelter, where Webster was adopted, whenever he can. He's reading every crime and detective novel he can get his hands on. He and Gracie text each other a lot. He's started to use his phone calendar to mark off the days until he sees Gracie again.

Gracie is doing well at school and has decided to continue her studies in pre-med. She's thinking of majoring in psychiatry, now that she's had a chance to expand her world. She texts Lucas a lot. Every once in a while she takes out one of Lucas's flannel plaid shirts that she "borrowed" and wears it to go to sleep. She smiles a lot now and looks forward to seeing Lucas on vacation.

Brent was sentenced to two years in juvenile detention

but was paroled after six months. He's in court-ordered individual therapy and family therapy with his dad, Matt. He has one year probation and one year of doing community service, where he mostly cleans up the parks. The fact that he did hire his cousin Ronald to scare Tucker came out at Ronald's trial, he just didn't know how far his crazy cousin would go. He is sorry for what he did and is working on his anger management. Tucker and Brent forgave each other and are friends again after a million sincere apologies from both of them. He is currently living with his mom, Karen, and her fiancé, Tom, who is a nice guy. Brent also lost his license to drive.

Jerry Morrison, twin to Matt, was proven innocent of all wrongdoing and bought, with his half of the sale of the mansion, a Used Car Dealership. He's happy as can be giving away gold pens that say "Morrisons Chapel and Crematorium" to any customer who buys a golden package used car deal.

Vicki and Brent broke up, and now she's dating the Fairfax High School star quarterback. She took Gracie's advice and applied to ten colleges.

Ronald Morrison was tried and convicted of kidnapping and arson and was sentenced to twenty years in prison, but after a scuffle with an inmate, he was transferred into a psych hospital to be evaluated. Mostly he spends his time polishing his dad's shoes, and he has taken up pottery. Matt writes and phones Ronald when he can.

Matt Morrison was arrested and charged with arson and

insurance fraud and sentenced to prison for three years with three years probation. He talks to Brent whenever he's allowed, and they are in therapy together. He wants to get a respectable job when he gets out and break ties with the Morrison family. He's in an anger management program in the prison.

Karen Morrison got a divorce from Matt and now has her own local TV show featuring Victorian decor with the designer who was parked in front of her house. They are engaged. She shares custody of Brent with Matt.

Toby Wallace retired from Morrison's before it was sold and became a local hero for trying to save the Morrison Chapel and Crematorium. He's always blamed himself for not being home to save his family in his house fire but now finally feels vindicated. He's helping out at a local grocery store and still smells like 100 cigarette butts.

Officer Morrow got a promotion. She's now Sergeant Morrow and is studying to be a detective in the police force.

Alex met a kindred spirit in creative writing class when she read her short story, "My Brother the Zombie." He loved her writing and her sense of humor. They are co-writing a teenage slasher film and currently looking for a director.

Gordy is happy hanging out with a girl he met in San Jose and is probably moving in with his dad for next year. He never gets tired of listening to Lucas tell him how he almost got murdered.

There was no actual reward for finding Tucker. But Tucker

and his family are forever beholden to Lucas and Gracie for never giving up their search.

The three unclaimed crematory urns are no longer unclaimed as they happily reside on the top shelf in Lucas's closet. Some nights Lucas swears he hears laughter coming from his closet, which is totally no big surprise to him.

The End...

Or Is It?